IF WE BREAK UP

CHEYANNE YOUNG

QUINNOVA
PRESS

IF WE BREAK UP

CHEYANNE YOUNG

Published by Quinnova Press
www.QuinnovaPress.com
www.CheyanneYoung.com

The text is set in Iowan Old Style
Edited by Cheyanne Young
Cover design by Cheyanne Young
Cover Images © Canva Pro

Young, Cheyanne, author
If We Break Up / Cheyanne Young.

ISBN: 978-0-578-35332-6 (Paperback)

For Susan Connally, world's best alpha reader & expert bottle opener.

CHAPTER ONE

"We are failing the Bechdel test right now."

At the sound of my voice, my best friend tears her gaze from Shawn Beck's backside, an act that is frankly a miracle, because she's just spent five minutes telling me all about how sexy those Varsity butt cheeks look in track shorts. Maggie lifts an eyebrow. "The *what?*"

A warm gust of wind blows my hair all in my face for the hundredth time since we sat down. I wanted to suggest that we study in the library, or at the snow cone place off Main Street, but today is a track meet day. Track meet days are always spent on the bleachers next to Maggie. I'm here to cheer on my boyfriend and she's here to check out the athletic eye candy. It's a tradition. You can't skip tradition. The foundation of my entire life is built upon traditions.

"The Bechdel test," I say, nudging her textbook with my knee to draw her attention back to the task at hand. The book is open on her lap, but she hasn't actually looked at it since we sat down ten minutes ago. "It's a theory that points out how in movies, every time there are two women together, they always talk about a guy. They're never talking about anything of substance, like quantum physics or curing cancer or something. It's *always* a guy. We're better than that, Mags."

"But talking about guys is *so* much more fun than physics… or homework." Her thick English accent is more pronounced when she's complaining. She sneaks one last glance at Shawn's butt as he leaps over a hurdle before reluctantly looking at her textbook, her bottom lip poking out in protest. "This stuff is so easy, love. Why do we have to keep going over it?"

"Because your smart techie brain understands all of this computer programming crap and my pathetic brain doesn't."

"Hey look! We're not talking about guys anymore." Maggie wiggles her eyebrows, throwing back her shoulders in this haughty way as her chin tilts toward the sky. "We have passed the Bechdel test."

"And you just ruined it by bringing up guys again!" I flatten my hands on top of my textbook. "Quiz me on the vocab words and then we can quit for the day."

"Fine."

We go through the vocabulary list ten times until I finally have it memorized. Our computer programming class was supposed to be an easy A elective class to fill out my senior year schedule, but it turned out to be less playing on the computer and more memorizing technical terms, thanks to the two jackass football players who poured an energy drink on the computer lab keyboards for their internet fans.

Maggie is not only one of the greatest teenage makeup artists on Instagram, she's also naturally skilled at all things technical. If she didn't study with me before most tests, I'd be nowhere near passing this boring class.

"Okay, where is that gorgeous boy…" Maggie says after

she shoves her textbook into her backpack. She leans forward, her eyes narrowing as they scan the track in front of us, searching for Shawn Beck. Today's track meet is smaller than usual, with only three nearby schools competing in the track and field events.

"He's in line for the boy's relay," I say, nodding toward to the field where Shawn stands next to Luca. They're both varsity track stars, in nearly all of the same events together, and they've been friends since junior high when Shawn moved here from Houston. I think this is part of the reason Maggie has such a huge crush on Shawn. He's Luca's best friend. And she's my best friend. It's a proximity crush.

"I need you to promise me something, Honey." Maggie rests her chin in her palm while she stares longingly at the tall, dark, and handsome object of her affection. "If school ends and I still haven't gotten the courage to ask him out, I need you to pull some strings. Maybe hint that I like him or something. I can't go off to NYC without having at least one date with him. He's *gorgeous*, Honey."

Her head tilts to the side and she's in full on boy crush mode. I expect her insides to come melting out of her any second now. "Can you imagine our little mixed-race children? They'd be so freaking cute. What if they got my curly dark hair and his perfect cheekbones?" She breathes in deeply and sighs, shaking her head slowly.

"So ask him out, already! Nothing's going to change if you don't make a move."

"It's not that easy." She shakes her head. "I'm not sure he even likes me? He's always making fun of my accent."

"I think that's just playful teasing, love," I say in my best imitation of her English accent. "Everyone thinks it's cool, Mags.

You sound more sophisticated than the rest of us small town Texas darlin's."

I say that last part with a thick southern drawl that I definitely don't have in real life, and it makes her laugh. Maggie moved here two years ago when her dad was promoted at a nearby architectural firm. In a town as small as Stonebrook, where everyone knows everyone and we're all just teeming with Southern Charm, a girl from England was a pretty big deal. It was the most exciting thing to happen in my sophomore year, and we all thought she was cool as hell. I still think she's cool as hell. I've never exactly had close girlfriends until Maggie came along.

Maggie's fingers wrap around my arm and she rests her head on my shoulder. Her massive curly hair most definitely gets in my mouth and I try to spit it out without her noticing. "You should ask Luca to put in a good word for me."

The aluminum bleachers wobble as two of our friends climb up to where we're sitting. Aidyn and Leigh are on the girl's track team, so they're dressed in matching Wildcats uniforms—dark blue shorts and silver tank tops with a large, ragged paw print on the front.

"Oh my *god*," Aidyn says as she drops down one bleacher seat below and turns to face us. "Jacob from Wimberly High is here and he is so freaking, unbelievably, undeniably, ridiculously, hot."

"Does anyone ever pass the Bechdel test?" Maggie asks, but I'm the only one who seems to notice.

"I think that guy from Klein Cain is hotter," Leigh says, untwisting the cap off her sports drink.

"Can we *please* talk about anything else besides guys?" I beg. "Why can't we talk about my moms' graduation parties or celebrity gossip or—literally, just anything else?"

"Honey is such a killjoy," Aidyn says, turning a snarky look to Leigh. "She's like this old married lady killjoy."

Leigh nods eagerly and Maggie nods right along with her. I throw her my most betrayed glare and she chuckles. "You don't care to talk about guys, Honey, because you already have the perfect guy. The rest of us aren't so lucky."

I sit up straighter. "I think if you like someone you should ask them out. Talking about it all day long isn't going to do anything."

Aidyn rolls her eyes. "That's easy for you to say. You've never had to ask anyone out."

"Has Luca always been this hot or did he grow into his looks after puberty?" Maggie asks, her eyes narrowing on the field as if she can decipher Luca's genetics through sight alone.

"A little bit of both," Leigh answers.

I don't know why it's bothering me, but I can feel my cheeks get warm as I twirl my moonstone ring around my index finger. It happens every single time my friends start talking about my hot boyfriend. I just want to throw up my arms and scream *I get it! He's hot! You don't have to keep saying it!*

I hold my tongue but it's not like it matters. Now that Luca has been brought up, my friends are all too happy to keep talking about him, comparing him with the other hot guys at our school as if I'm not sitting here being forced to listen to it.

If you were to cut Luca out of real life and cast him as the star in a Netflix original teen romance, then yeah, I'd binge watch every episode, because at face value, my boyfriend *is* hot. But when I look at him, I don't see the forearm muscles Maggie raves about or the tall, muscular athlete who won the Cutest Couple superlative with me last month.

When I look at Luca, I see that jagged scar on his lip from the time we climbed too high in the tree behind Nana's backyard and he fell down trying to reach for my hand so I wouldn't be scared. I see the golden brown eyes that widened in horror when I got my first period while playing X-box on the floor of his game room when we were twelve and his parents weren't home and he handed me maxi pads from his mom's bathroom and said, "Here, I think this is what you need."

When I look at Luca, I don't just see my boyfriend. I see my childhood. My best friend. Every birthday party and every Christmas and every single holiday from the day I was born. I don't get all swoony-eyed and boy crazy like everyone else seems to get when they're around him. When I look at Luca, I no longer see all his good qualities. All I see lately is the person holding me back from going after the only thing I want in this life.

The fake pistol pops, sending a poof of smoke into the air and the boys' relay race begins. My friends stop gushing over the guys and focus on the track instead. The Wildcats track team is Stonebrook High's only claim to fame. Luca is the last one in the relay race, like always. He has enough speed to shave off a few seconds if his teammates are lagging behind the other team.

Someone's dad cheers from the sidelines as he walks up the bleachers, a toddler holding onto one hand while he balances a box of pizza in the other. They walk right past us and sit a few rows back. The smell of the pizza lingers in the air until a breeze carries it away, but by then it's too late. I've been reminded of something my aunt Bree said last year. And now the very thought of it burrows into my thoughts, taking all my attention away from Luca's relay race.

Aunt Bree is eight years younger than my mom, and she's always felt more like a slightly older best friend than my aunt. She's a stunning six-foot-tall woman with long golden-brown hair and—I kid you not—a perfect little mole on her right cheek. She lucked out in life, somehow getting just the beautiful traits from my grandparent's DNA and none of the bad ones. I bet she could have been a model if she wanted. Instead of marrying and having kids, she decided to stay blissfully single and travel the world.

Last summer when she returned home from months in Italy, she and I stayed up until three in the morning looking at all the photos she'd taken and hadn't yet posted to Instagram. Almost a hundred of them were shot from the balcony of a pizza place that was next door to her Airbnb. I remember so clearly how Aunt Bree had described Italian pizza.

A "true" Italian pizza is simple: paper-thin crust, fresh marinara sauce, and slabs of mozzarella topped with a sprig of fresh basil—nothing else. She said the pizzeria's stone oven had been baking pizza for centuries so all the thousands of pizzas that came before this one had worked together to season the oven, which in turn gave the crust a delicious, irreplaceable flavor that we in the States would never ever experience. Because our pizza ovens aren't that old yet.

The way Aunt Bree described this pizza had my mouth watering, and if there had been enough money in my bank account, I might have bought a round trip flight to Italy right then and there to I could eat the pizza myself. When I told her that, she laughed. She said the thing about the most amazing pizza you've ever had is that it's only earth-shatteringly good the first few times you eat it. Since she was staying next door, she'd eaten there nearly every day. By the last day of her trip, she took a bite of that golden crust, and while it was still just as perfect as all the pizzas she'd eaten before, somehow, she'd felt a bit of her passion for it slipping away. After a while, tasting this pizza wasn't the same life-altering out-of-body experience because she'd grown used to it.

After a while, it was just pizza.

"Go Wildcats!" Aidyn yells, letting out a whoop of triumph. "That's what I'm talking about!"

Looks like our team took another win. Luca drops the relay bar and then pulls off his track jersey, using it to wipe the sweat from his face. He turns toward the bleachers, his eyes zoning in right to where I'm sitting. He blows a kiss.

Something inside of me recoils. It hasn't always been this way. I've been pathetically in love with my boyfriend for most of my life. These last few months have changed everything. It started when I got my college acceptance letter.

Not the acceptance to Texas A&M, which is both our parents' alma matter and the college we've always known we'd be attending...getting into that university was a given. My acceptance to Fault Line University was unexpected. It's my dream school. My long shot. The Hail Mary application I sent off just to pay homage to the type of girl I'd like to be. The girl who breaks tradition and goes out of state to pursue my dream instead of staying home and working at the family business with Luca.

"Is he coming over here?" Leigh asks as Luca jogs across the track, heading our way.

"I think so."

"Tell him to bring all his hot friends," Maggie says with a laugh. "And by hot friends, I mean Shawn."

"Don't take this the wrong way," Aidyn says, her hand touching my arm. "But your boyfriend looks like a Greek god."

"*Mmmhmm,*" Leigh says.

Maggie nods. "You're so lucky." That statement earns her a round of agreement from our friends.

I love Maggie, but I really wish she would shut up. I wish everyone would shut up. I don't need to be reminded about how supposedly lucky I am. I get it. I really do.

My smile is reluctant, but I shove it in place as Luca takes the bleacher steps two at a time, the afternoon sunshine glistening off his sweat-covered abs. Yeah, he's gorgeous. He's got muscles for days and forearm veins that should be photographed in black and white and plastered on a billboard. His jawline could cut glass, and those piercing azure eyes are the color of a stormy ocean that makes you want to dive right in.

"Congrats on the win," I say, tilting my head up.

He places a quick kiss on my lips. "Thanks."

All three of my friends are staring at him, but he doesn't seem to notice. I notice. I'm not sure if I'm feeling annoyed or just really guilty.

Luca is my built-in date to every school event. My best friend. My other half. Maggie is right. What more could a girl ask for?

But now, when my friends are giving me serious jealous vibes, and the girls' track team is staring daggers at me from the sidelines, I get this weird little knot in my stomach. This acute ache that starts off small and then widens, bigger and bigger, until all I can think about is how it doesn't matter how delicious it is… sometimes a pizza is just a pizza.

And when it comes to my ultra-hot boyfriend? Sometimes he's just a guy. A guy standing in the way of my dream college. He doesn't know I was accepted into FLU. I haven't told him, or my parents, or anyone. In our families, you don't break tradition. Tradition is here in Texas, going to A&M and then working at the greatest construction business this small town has ever seen. Tradition is not in Colorado.

That ache in my chest tightens and I can't seem to make it go away.

Then it happens.

I glance over at Luca and it's like I'm not even seeing him clearly. For the first time in my entire life, I want to break up.

CHAPTER TWO

Rollins & Blackwell Construction is the second largest employer in our small town, right after the grocery store. I've spent most of my life here since the business opened a few months after I was born. The dads do remodeling, construction, and custom projects while the moms are the most well-known real estate agents in the county. I only have one mom and dad, but my parents are lifelong best friends, neighbors, and business partners with Luca's parents. We live next door to the Rollins and I've known them my whole life, so in a way, I have two sets of parents. Luca and I just call them "the moms" and "the dads."

My mom does most of the actual real estate paperwork and Luca's mom, Jill, is more into staging homes and taking photography for the listings. All of the R&B Realty For Sale signs feature a picture of the moms, their backs together in a classic "we're a team" pose. One day when I'm an official licensed Realtor, they will no doubt redo the signs with me in the middle.

The front desk is empty when Luca and I get to work on

Saturday morning. This modern front desk was the brainchild of the moms a few years ago, after R&B had been hit with a particularly bad review online. Someone had walked into the office wanting to sell their house, but no one was up front to greet them, and although you can clearly see Mom and Jill working in their offices across the lobby thanks to the floor-to-ceiling glass walls, this person decided to walk right back outside and type a nasty review.

Two weeks later, this sleek custom desk was installed. They hired Maddison to sit behind the desk as the official company receptionist. Unfortunately for me, Maddison actually does get weekends off and I have to fill in for her when my parents decide to work.

"I'm needed in the shop," Luca says, slipping an arm around my waist in a quick hug. "Love you."

Luca's forehead has this slight little crease right down the middle between his brows. It's faint, but almost identical to the deeper one in his dad's forehead. The two men look so similar, both broad-shouldered, with dark auburn hair. Both have light colored skin that tans easily (and is always tan due to working outside), and both have that little forehead wrinkle. When I look at Tony Rollins it's like I'm seeing Luca in the future. I wonder if Luca thinks the same thing about me when he sees my mom.

That faint crease in his forehead deepens. "What's wrong...?"

"Huh?" I say, then I quickly add, "Nothing."

One anti-perk of having dated the same guy your entire life is that he knows everything about you. He demonstrates this now by giving me a look. "Something's wrong."

I roll my eyes and smile and push away that clawing guilt in my stomach that grows angrier each day I keep my FLU acceptance a secret. "Nothing is wrong. I was just distracted." Luca is a good eight inches taller than I am so I have to lift up on my toes to kiss him on the cheek. "Love you, too."

He doesn't push the issue and I watch him walk through the clean lobby that smells faintly of coconut sunshine, or whatever summery wax is in the warmer today, and slip out the double doors that lead into the warehouse.

I'm jealous he gets to work the construction side of the job, working with tools and lumber and paint and sheetrock, while I'm stuck here answering phones and posting on R&B's Facebook page as the unofficial social media manager.

I slink into Maddison's buttery soft leather office chair. Dad bought it for her after she complained about getting back pain from the original chair. It's probably the nicest office chair in existence—all soft and plush and huge. Closing my eyes, I lean my head back and spin the chair around just for fun.

When my eyes open I realize I'm not alone. An older woman with silvery hair tied into a tight bun is sitting in one of the waiting chairs against the wall. She looks vaguely familiar, but then again, everyone in Stonebrook knows everyone else in some small way. Her lips crinkle into a grin.

"You two are the most adorable couple."

"Aren't they the cutest?" Jill appears, holding a manila folder. She flashes me a warm, deep red-lipsticked smile. "I always knew they'd fall in love one day, but I had no idea how cute they'd be together. Here are the comps for your house, Mrs. Beck."

Ah, that's how I know her. She's Shawn's grandmother. Volunteer for every single PTA event from kindergarten through high school.

The older woman thanks Jill for the paperwork and then

turns to me. "I wish Shawn would find a nice girl like you. He spends too much time playing video games when he could be out dating and making something of himself."

I bite the inside of my lip. I could easily tell her that my best friend has a huge crush on her grandson, but I'm not about to go spilling Maggie's personal business all over the place. "Maybe I'll set him up with one of my friends," I say instead.

Mrs. Beck nods. "That would be wonderful."

After she leaves, Jill turns to me with an overly exaggerated look of exhaustion. "I'm so ready to go home," she says, sprawling her arms over the desk like she's about to pass out. "I've been here since six! On a freaking Saturday!"

I glance back toward the hallway where I can just see the edge of my mom's profile through her office window wall, where she's diligently at work on her computer. "What was so important that we all had to come in to work today?"

"Hell if I know," she says, rolling her eyes. "We have some new listings and Amber just couldn't wait until Monday. I love your mom, but she works way too hard."

Although they've been best friends since they were little kids, my mom and Jill are opposites in so many ways. Mom is a perfectionist, soft spoken, and really into following all the rules. I have *never* seen my mom drunk, even though she sips wine with Jill every single weekend around our backyard firepit. Jill is the carefree one, just like her son. She's always in a good mood. Even when she's complaining about work, she finds a way to do it in an upbeat way. I can't help but think that she would be on board with me going to Colorado. I wish I could tell her. I wish I could tell my parents.

I wish I could tell Luca.

Jill perches on the edge of the desk and reaches out,

running her fingers through my hair. "So what's up in teenager world? Ya'll got big plans for tonight?"

"I don't think so," I say, turning slightly so she'll play with more of my hair. The great thing about my life with Luca is that I basically have two moms and two dads. Lately I've felt closer with Luca's mom than my own mom. "Maybe I'll kick Luca out of the house tonight so we can finish binge watching our show."

"Ooh, now that's a good idea!" Jill says. How easily she can betray her own son when it comes to a handsome fictional hitman on the big screen TV. She laughs and gathers my hair into one hand, then divides it in thirds and twists it into a loose braid. "I better get back to work before your mom slaughters me."

Alone once again, I lean back in Maddison's chair and scroll through the business Facebook page. The dads have a reputation for posting these cheesy videos of themselves giving home improvement advice in an attempt to get more follows and likes. They are both terrible actors, but you can't argue with the results. In our town of six thousand people, they have forty thousand Facebook fans.

My phone rings and Aunt Bree's name pops up on the screen. "Hey," I say, pressing the phone to my ear while I spin around in Maddison's chair. "What's up?"

"Honey Bun. I have brookies."

"Ughhhhh. I'm stuck at work," I whine, tossing my head back. Brookies are Aunt Bree's dessert specialty, consisting of brownie mix and cookie batter all baked into one delicious brookie that we eat straight out of the pan with scoops of vanilla ice cream on top. Gorging ourselves on the sugary monstrosity is our tradition when she comes back home from another one of her worldly adventures.

"I'll keep it warm for you."

"You're the best."

"Psh, I know."

When work is over, Luca drives me to Aunt Bree's apartment. He knows these brookie dates with Aunt Bree are more of a girls' only thing, but I still feel bad that I don't invite him to come up with me. All this guilt I have over keeping my college secret is seeping into every other aspect of our relationship.

He parks in front of Stonebrook's only laundromat, which is right below Aunt Bree's studio apartment. "When do you need me to pick you up?"

"I don't know. I'll text you?"

His smile is soft and sweet and totally oblivious to the whirlwind of thoughts wreaking havoc in my mind. "Cool."

I head inside the empty laundromat and walk to the back where an *employees only* sign hangs on the door that leads to the narrow stairwell that goes up to my aunt's apartment. The owner of the laundromat used to live up here but then he died, (not in the apartment, luckily) and his daughter took over the business and rented it to Aunt Bree. They were dating at the time, but after they broke up they stayed friends and my aunt got to keep renting the place.

I was really worried when I first found out that they were splitting up. Stonebrook is smaller than small, and there's not exactly a bustling apartment complex nearby. This little laundromat apartment might be the only one-bedroom place to rent in town, and it's what keeps my aunt here, near her family when she's not traveling. I don't know what I'd do if I didn't get to see her every few weeks. She's the only member of my family who lives as freely as I wish I could.

"There she is," Aunt Bree says when she opens the door.

She salutes me with her glass of wine. "My little college-bound niece. I'm so proud of you."

"Huh?" I step past her slim figure and wander into the kitchen in search of the brookie. "I've always been college-bound."

The studio apartment only has two rooms: the bathroom, and the rest of the place. A kitchen area is on the far wall, and Aunt Bree's antique wooden dining table separates the area into the living room, which has just the one fluffy denim couch. Across from that is her bed, which is piled high with colorful pillows and a patchwork quilt that she made herself from different hand-dyed fabrics she bought in India.

My aunt prefers handmade, eclectic décor that she's collected from her travels over cheap mass-produced crap like the décor we use to stage the homes we sell. She's a freelance graphic designer, but she's friends with artists from all over the globe. Their artwork hangs on the walls.

Last year she briefly dated this guy named Thom, who painted photo-realistic canvases of people and landscapes. His art was some of the best I've ever seen, and the painting of Aunt Bree sitting on the kitchen counter, sipping wine with one hand while painting her toes with the other still hangs on the wall. It's right where a normal person would put a TV, but my aunt doesn't have one—she says she's never home long enough to justify it. I had begged the moms to buy some of Thom's art so we could stage homes with it, but they both said no. Houses are supposed to be staged in basic, boring color schemes so potential buyers can visualize their stuff in the home.

That's just another reason I don't want to be a real estate agent. Basic and boring is not fun.

"Coffee table," Aunt Bree says.

I turn away from the small kitchen area and find the brookie in a glass baking dish with an opened carton of vanilla ice cream that has two spoons stuck in the top. I grab one of the spoons and plonk down on the couch. Aunt Bree doesn't join me. She just stands there, this weird-ass look on her face.

"What?" I say. A sinister tingle creeps up my spine. I haven't done anything wrong—I'm not in trouble. So why is she staring at me like this?

"Why haven't you told me you're getting out of this dumbass town?" She plants her hands on her hips. "Hell, maybe I'll move to Colorado too."

My skin turns cold. "How do you know about Colorado?"

She bends down to the MacBook that's open on her coffee table, spinning it around to face me. The browser is open to an email platform. My email.

Right there at the very top of my inbox is that one Fault Line University email I haven't been strong enough to delete. But can you blame me? How do you delete something that basically says: *Congratulations, you could actually do something with your life!*

"I guess you logged in when you were over here last time," she says, finally sitting next to me. "I take my iPad travelling, so I only just saw it when I got home."

Heat floods into my cheeks. She was never supposed to know this. Aunt Bree would keep a secret for me, no matter how dark or twisted or awful. I know she would. But this secret is mine. It's not dark or twisted or awful. It's a good secret, which makes everything worse.

I shake my head and stare at the cold spoon in my fingers. "I can't go. I don't even know why I applied."

"Excuse you?" Aunt Bree folds herself onto the overstuffed denim couch and points her spoon at me. "Why can't you go?

You've been accepted! If you need money, there are student loans, and I could help you—I have some savings—"

"No, it's not that." I shrug. "Or maybe it is that? I don't know. I didn't think about any of that. I never thought I'd get in."

"Of course you got in! You're brilliant, Bun." Her words are too happy, too blissfully upbeat. Too eager to see me leave this town and do something unexpected of me, probably so she won't be the only black sheep of the family.

I don't say anything. Instead, I lean forward and stare at the brookie, willing myself to be as excited to eat it now as I was a few minutes ago. It smells amazing, but my stomach is a solid rock.

"I did some research, kid. This school is legit. You'd be right in the middle of nature, learning about the earth instead of being stuffed into some stupid, cold, fluorescent-lit building in Texas." She takes a long sip of wine, her gaze piercing into me the whole time. "This college is you. It's *so* you. You love nature. You love science. Why the hell aren't you going?"

Finally giving up on the dessert, I drop the spoon and run my fingers over my eyebrows. "You know why I can't go."

"No, Honey. I don't."

I give her a look that says *yes you do*.

But my aunt is as stubborn as she is beautiful and she just stares right back at me for the longest few seconds. She's going to make me say it.

"I can't leave Luca."

Her gaze doesn't change, so I have to step up my excuses. It's easy to name them all—I've been doing it in my head for weeks. "I'm already accepted at A&M. I can't leave the family business, Aunt Bree. You know this. I have to get my real estate license. Dad is already cleaning out space from the storage closet at R&B to build my own office. I will take over Mom's job one day and Luca will take over his dad's job and that's just how it will be. There's no room for an out-of-state college in the middle of that."

"There is always room for college."

I sit up a little straighter. Aunt Bree is usually the cool one, the person I turn to when I need advice that's not too motherly or grown up. But right now she's giving off serious parental vibes and I'm not okay with it. "I have to get my real estate license. Being a geophysicist will not help me sell houses."

That stern expression slides right off her face. I thought I hated that look but the one that replaces it is worse. Pity.

"Bun..." She draws in a slow breath, staring at the wine glass clasped in her hands. "When will you start living for yourself?"

"I do live for myself," I grumble.

"Do you?" She snorts, shaking her head a bit as she gazes at a family photo on the wall. "My sister and her best friend are obsessed with doing everything together. They found boyfriends and got married together. They had kids together. They put the two of you to work at the family business when you were *toddlers*. You've spent your whole life thinking you have to follow in their footsteps, but Honey, you don't."

"I want to," I say, even as the moment the words leave my mouth, I know I don't really believe them. I don't truly want to work at R&B my whole life, but what Aunt Bree is saying is practically heresy. I don't even want to picture the look on my mom's face if I told her I didn't want to work alongside her after graduation. It would gut her. It would gut both moms and both dads. All of their hard work creating a life for us would have been for nothing.

"I have a job lined up for me after graduating from A&M. I'd be stupid not to take it."

"So fine, be a real estate agent," she says. "But go to college first and then come back and do that. You're so young and you have your whole life to work at R&B."

"I can't just leave for four years."

She rolls her eyes. "What the hell is stopping you? And don't say Luca. I love the kid, but he's not worth it if he's gonna chain you down to this stupid town. What did he say about it?"

"Nothing. I haven't told him. I haven't told anyone, because this doesn't matter."

Aunt Bree reaches over and grabs my hand. Her skin is soft and smells faintly of vanilla lotion. "Talk to that boy of yours. He loves you, and he'll help you figure it out. Together you can find a way to tell your parents that you're going to college."

"You think so?" I ask. My voice is filled with this fresh and vibrant hope, a kind of hope I haven't had at all since getting that acceptance email.

Aunt Bree's long thin lips press into a sardonic smirk. "Bun. It's Luca. You know he will do anything for you."

CHAPTER THREE

Welp. This is happening. I'm going to ask Luca to help me convince my parents to let me go to college in Colorado.

And I'm going to wing it.

"Talk to that boy of yours. He loves you, and he'll help you figure it out."

I'm too late for Jill's Sunday morning waffles, but the smell of maple syrup lingers in the air in Luca's house. His German Shephard is the first to notice me when I let myself into their kitchen from the backdoor. Rudo's tail wags happily when he sees me, and he rushes over for some ear scratches. I wish I could stay here and pet the dog forever but there's only a few weeks until the deadline to accept my college acceptance.

I snort to myself as I debate spending the next few weeks petting Rudo and ignoring my responsibilities. It would be a hell of a lot more fun and I don't think Rudo would complain.

"Luca?" I call out. Might as well get this over with.

"He's out front," Jill calls back from somewhere in the house. "Washing his truck."

I venture into the living room and find her and Luca's dad

watching TV while they work on a puzzle on the coffee table. His dad is sitting on the floor, squinting at the pieces.

"That's what I get for going through the backyard," I say with a weak laugh. I'm trying to act extremely normal but I fear I'm failing.

Jill smiles and places a corner piece of the puzzle. "I saved you a waffle in the fridge. Just microwave it for a few seconds and it should be good."

"Thanks." I'm far too nervous to eat, but she doesn't need to know that.

Outside, Luca is shirtless and barefoot, wearing board shorts while he hoses off his truck, a bucket of suds on the driveway next to him. "Hey, beautiful," he says over the rushing spray of water from the hose.

"Hey, hot stuff."

He kneels down and starts scrubbing the grime off his wheels. "You still in a brookie hangover?"

Those are the words I'd used last night when he picked me up from Aunt Bree's. Too many thoughts were flooding my mind and I needed time to sort through them, so I'd faked a stomachache so we didn't have to hang out.

"I'm better now," I say.

"Good, because I missed you."

My heart squeezes at his sweet words. I watch him, his tanned skin in the sunlight, his muscles flexing as he washes his truck, a cleaning effort he's only making because I'd complained about his dirty truck the other day. Luca is great. I don't know why I thought about breaking up with him. He loves me, and he'll support me. I just need to get this college confession over with.

"Can we go somewhere when you're done?" I ask, shielding the bright morning sun with my hand.

"Sure. Where to?"

"Anywhere."

He glances at me curiously and then moves to the next wheel, dragging his soap bucket beside him. "Dog park?"

I smile. "Perfect."

Rudo is nearly ten years old, which makes him seventy in dog years, but he acts like a puppy every time we bring him to the dog park. Luca unhooks the leash and lets him run free around the small man-made pond. He slings an arm around my shoulders while we walk. His steps are leisurely, but my whole body is tense.

"I shampooed the inside of my truck," he says, tossing Rudo's foam ball back into the pond for him to fetch again. "Now it won't smell like old track uniforms."

"Finally," I say with a snort. His truck has been smelling like a locker room for days.

Luca pulls back, those deep blue eyes looking into mine. "You okay?"

He knows me as well as I know myself. I'm doing my best acting here, but I'm surprised it took him this long to pick up that I'm a little off today.

"Yes," I say, my voice sure. "I do need to talk to you, though. But it's good news."

"Okay..." Rudo brings the ball back and Luca takes it, then hurls it to the far side of the pond. "What's your good news?"

I gnaw on the inside of my lip. My plan to wing it is officially in action.

"So... that Colorado college? Um…. I got in."

Luca stops walking. Rudo runs up to us, tail wagging as he sets the ball at Luca's feet. His human doesn't notice it because he's too busy staring at me. I know all of Luca's expressions—his happy ones, his sad ones. I know the look he gets when someone says something that could totally be a "that's what she said" joke but he can't say anything because adults are around. I know every face he's ever made, but I haven't seen this one before.

His lips flatten, and then he says, slowly and carefully, "What does that mean?"

"My dream school," I say quickly putting on a bright smile so he'll know that this is supposed to be fun and exciting. "They accepted me. I got in."

"I heard *what* you said, but I don't understand why you said it."

Rudo's tail stops wagging. He looks at us with eager puppy eyes and I bend down and take the ball, then throw it. "I know it's not exactly the plan, but I really want to go."

"You want to leave me and go to another state for four years?"

"No," I say, grabbing his arm. "I was thinking you could come with me."

Actually, I wasn't thinking that. I don't know what I was thinking. *Winging It* is officially the *Worst Plan Ever*.

"And I'm supposed to do what in Colorado?" Luca scoffs. "Sleep in your dorm room like some kind of house pet?"

"Luca, no… you could get a job or something."

"I have a job!" Luca pulls his arm from my grasp and takes a step back. Rudo drops the ball at Luca's feet and he kicks it so hard it soars right over the lake and lands in a bush.

"Luca…"

He cuts me off with a sharp shake of his head. "You have a job too, Honey. You're supposed to get your real estate license."

"I can still do that," I say defensively. "Just after I graduate from FLU."

"I'm not leaving R&B," he says. "You know my dad can't work much longer. He doesn't have four years left for me to jet off to Colorado. I can't believe you would do this to me. To him. He's practically your dad, too."

A bitter, awful guilt sinks in my stomach. In all my excitement over being accepted to my dream college, I hadn't even thought about Luca's dad. Two years ago, he discovered his glaucoma had progressed so much that eye drops and surgery wouldn't help him anymore. The doctors have given him only a few years until he loses his sight completely.

What was I thinking? Luca can't leave home. He has to take over for his dad. He *wants* to take over for his dad.

"I… I'm sorry," I say, dropping my head. "I forgot about your dad's vision."

"You forgot about a lot of things, apparently. Like me. And your family. And our future. How could you do this to us?"

Tears pool in my eyes. "I know it's crazy, but this is my dream school, and it's only four years. We can figure this out together."

He bends down and throws Rudo's ball. When he turns back to me, his eyes are watery. "What is there to figure out? You go off to college and what? I spend every dime I have flying up to see you once a month?"

I gnaw on my lip. "We'll take turns flying to each other. I'll be home every summer and I'll come home for every long weekend, I promise."

I can tell he's thinking it over, playing out the idea of it in his mind, and it only encourages me to keep talking. "It's just four years, babe. We've been together for eighteen. Four years will be nothing."

"It's not just four years, though. It's college. I'll be at

A&M. How am I supposed to have a fun college life when you're not there with me?"

I don't know how to answer that because now I'm visualizing it. Luca, with his gorgeous face and heart-melting smile, at some college party with everyone tossing flirty looks his way. Luca, hanging out on campus without me. Me, in Colorado with exactly zero friends.

Rudo gruffs his annoyance at our feet but Luca doesn't acknowledge the old dog. My mouth opens and then it just stays there, frozen like this because I can't think of anything to say.

His eyes flicker. I've lost him. "There's no way that would work."

Rudo gruffs again. I grab his ball and fling it as far as I can, then I turn back to Luca. "Can we please try? I want to go to FLU. I want this degree."

Luca flinches. "I thought you wanted me."

"I do," I say. "Of course I do." My voice cracks.

Luca's jaw tightens, his gaze cutting me like glass. I wish I could go back in time and take it all back. But I can't. It's out there now. The truth is hanging in the air between us, hidden in the space between the words I just said.

I know he heard that trace of doubt in my voice. It was impossible to miss.

He blinks quickly and looks away, his expression full of disbelief and... anger? "You know what, Honey? Do whatever the hell you want. I don't care."

"Luca..." I reach for him but he steps out of the way.

"Don't touch me. Don't try to make this right."

Rudo drops to the grass and chews on his ball.

"Please, Luca. Let's talk about this."

"There's nothing else to talk about. You're leaving me.

You're leaving the family. I thought you loved me, but apparently you don't." He throws his arms up, walking a few paces away before turning sharply back around. A bitter realization flashes across his face. "Did you bring me out here to break up with me?"

"What? No!" Tears flood my eyes. I reach for his arm, hoping to convince him that none of this is going the way I'd hoped, but he steps back and grabs Rudo's ball. The sinking feeling in my gut tells me he avoided my touch on purpose.

"You applied to that college before Christmas," Luca says, his jaw tightening. "How long have you kept this from me? Was this your plan all along? Just wait until graduation and leave me?"

"Luca..." I put my hand on his chest and peer up into his eyes, wishing he would see the truth in them. "I didn't plan anything. I wasn't expecting to get into FLU but I did and...I thought I could somehow make it work. *We* can make this work."

"I don't want to," he says, his voice so soft it blends into the breeze. "I want you, here with me. And if you don't want that then..."

I blink and tears roll down my cheeks.

Talk to that boy of yours. He loves you, and he'll help you figure it out.

Aunt Bree's words are on repeat in my mind. I hear her voice encouraging me to trust Luca to help me achieve what I want. She believed it, and I did too. I can't remember a time in my life where being next to Luca didn't bring me a sense of comfort and security. He's the one person on this earth that I trust to catch me if I close my eyes and fall. Now, for the first time in all eighteen years of my existence, I can feel that once-strong cord of trust starting to fray. Luca and I have argued before. We've called each other names and disagreed about this or that over the years. Which movie to watch, which shirt looks best, if a friend is fun or annoying.

But we've never, ever, fought like this.

That muscle in his jaw flexes again and he looks at me with eyes that have never quite looked at me like this before. This vast black hole between us is fresh new ground, a place we've never navigated, not in all of our years together. It's an uncharted territory.

Enemy territory.

CHAPTER FOUR

Luca gives me the silent treatment. An entire week goes by. We ride to school barely talking. We sit at lunch barely talking, and then we go home or to work and barely talk. I've tried bringing up our inevitable reunion, but the words always die on my tongue. Luca and I aren't some magical perfect couple, and we certainly aren't as amazing as our parents. We fight. We argue. It happens all the time. But it's never lasted this long.

I'm lying in bed, so impossibly wide awake that I almost forget what it feels like to be tired. My body is exhausted from this past week of quiet, awkward tension with Luca, but my mind is unable to shut off.

I squish up my pillow and roll over onto my side. The new position doesn't help me fall asleep. I check my phone, play some games, and scroll through social media, falling down the virtual rabbit hole of gemstone videos on Instagram. I should have unfollowed Fault Line University weeks ago.

Their newest post shows hundreds of large rocks the seniors collected over the past few weeks. The tradition is that freshmen choose a rock—they call it a boulder even though it's only about the size of a bag of sugar—and then hike it up to the top of a small mountain. You write your name on the rock and leave it there until you graduate, when you go back to find it. Every student does it. There's even a wheelchair-accessible trail to the top of the mountain.

I get lost watching posts of this years' seniors finding their rocks. Two hours pass and I'm still unable to fall asleep. Something has to give. Luca and I need to talk. This last week has been weirder than weird. We are not like this. We fight and we make up. But this time... the fight is lingering, hovering in the air, a mushroom cloud that won't dissipate.

I sit up, shoving the blankets off me as if they're the reason I'm uncomfortable. Scrubbing my hands over my face, I will myself to get tired.

Then I hear a soft cough coming from down the hall. It sounds like my mom, and it's close enough to be upstairs. My parents' bedroom is downstairs. I'm the only person who lives up here, and usually the only person who ever comes upstairs. I get up and walk to my door, peering out into the darkened hallway. A soft glow flickers off the wall, coming from our completely unused guest bedroom. Sometimes my grandparents stay over, but no one has been in there in months.

"Mom?" I say, padding softly down the hall.

I find her sitting on the guest bed, remote control in her hand. She's flipping through TV shows on Netflix. "Hi, Hon."

My hand rests on the door frame. "What are you doing?"

"Just watching TV."

"At two in the morning?"

Mom shrugs.

"The living room TV is better." The one up here is smaller and much older. My parents upgraded back when I was in junior high, and the old living room TV was dumped up here in the guest room. I don't even remember the last time it was turned on.

"It's too loud," she says, scrolling through film options in the Romantic Comedy section. "Don't wanna wake up Dad."

"Okay…" I know my mother is quite aware that our living room TV has a volume option, just like every TV in the history of the world. This is weird, but I don't press her for answers. Mom and I haven't been too close lately. She's always so focused on work and training me to take over for her. I've been avoiding chatting with her ever since I got accepted into FLU because all Mom ever wants to talk about is my future at the company.

She's not like Jill, who leaves work at the office when she leaves R&B each day. Jill can relax, turn off her work brain, and turn on her weekend brain to have fun. My mom used to be able to have fun, but not lately. Now she's just all about work.

I back away and leave her to her middle of the night Netflix binge.

"Honey?" she calls out softly.

I turn back, a little unsure if she actually called my name or if I'd imagined it. "Yeah, Mom?"

"How's school?" she asks. She offers me this half smile that makes me wonder if she's asking because she wants to or because she feels obligated.

"It's fine. I'm glad it's almost over."

She nods once. "How's Maggie?"

"She's great." My shoulders tense. I worry that her next question will be how's Luca, and even if we don't talk much lately, she can always tell when I'm lying. I decide to take over the conversation, steering it away from the well-being of the people in my social circle. "Hey, Mom? What do you do when you have a problem and you can't decide the best solution?"

She sets down the remote and tilts her head. Mom's face is narrow, with a sharp chin just like mine. Her hair is the same shade of brown, but mine is only the same dark shade on the top half of my hair. The rest of it is several shades lighter from having spent all of last summer outside.

"That's too general of a question," she says after considering it for a moment. "If it's a problem with work, I do what's best for the company. If it's a problem with cooking dinner, well, I'm not that great of a cook as you know, so I never come up with a solution."

I snort because she's right about that. Mom's cooking sucks. "Say you want to do something with the company, but Dad thinks your ideas are stupid, but you think his ideas are stupid. What do you do?"

Her expression darkens for just a split second. Or maybe it was just a trick of the light from the television playing the trailer for some new movie. "Is your father doing something to the company?"

I shake my head. "No, that was a dumb example."

It's late, and I'm so mentally drained from worrying about this Luca thing all week that I can't come up with a better example. One that says *how do you decide if you should break up with your boyfriend or not* without using those exact words. "I'm just wondering what you do when you don't know what to do?"

Mom uncrosses her legs, stretching them out on the bed. "Follow your heart."

"What if... what if it's more technical than that? What if there are too many details at play and you can't just follow your heart?"

Mom lifts an eyebrow. "Are you going to tell me the details of this problem you have?"

I shake my head. She chuckles. "I didn't think so."

"So what do I do?" I ask.

"Well... if you can't follow your heart, and you can't confide in your mother," she says, giving me a brisk look, "You could always try Google."

I waste another half hour in bed with my eyes closed, wishing sleep would come and take me away. When it's clear that sleep has no such plans for me, I open my laptop. Maybe I'll take my mom's sarcastic advice to heart. Maybe the all-knowing expertise of the World Wide Web will help me solve this problem.

The webpage loads, my cursor blinking in the search box. My teeth wear into my bottom lip as I consider what I want to search for. The very idea of putting my thoughts into words, seeing them on the screen, right there in pixels, instead of kept safely in my mind, sends a shiver down my body. Am I really going to do this?

Just to be safe, I open an incognito browser.

My fingers hover over the keyboard, the glowing keys bright in my dark room. I know the words. I know the question I want answered. I just can't believe this is happening. I take a deep breath and type:

Should I break up with my boyfriend?

Google has over two hundred and seventy million search results. I sink my chin into my palm as I scroll through endless pages of websites that all offer advice on the situation.

I can't read two hundred and seventy million websites. Closing my eyes, I click on a random search result.

A twenty-year research study is complete: The average person finds their soulmate after being in five relationships.

I lean in closer to the screen. This isn't some click-bait for a trashy magazine. It's a real scientific research study conducted by students at a prestigious university. They studied people who had been in long term, happy relationships for at least twenty years and who had no likelihood of getting divorced. The overwhelming majority of all the subjects had been in several relationships before finding "the one."

"While there are certainly outlying instances of a couple falling in love with their high school sweetheart and staying married until they die, that is an extreme rarity," the lead researcher, doctoral student Marta Channing said. "You're more likely to be struck by lightning than find true love in your first relationship. There is, however, overwhelming evidence that suggests there is a magic number of partners one must have before finding their true soulmate. That number is five."

Well, I think. *You can't argue with science.*

Fewer than one percent of the thousands of couples in this study were high school sweethearts who were still together. I glance out of my door, seeing the glow of the television flickering in the hallway. Maybe my parents and Luca's parents are that tiny minority, that exception to the rule. Luca and I grew up thinking we'd have the same long and happy relationship as well, but what are the odds that three couples from the same family would all fall into that one percent? I'm no statistician, but I know it's slim. Slimmer than slim.

Maybe even impossible.

The morning sunlight filters in through my bedroom window. The smell of coffee is faint way up here on the second floor, or maybe I'm just used to it. My parents can't start the day without the stuff so the scent is basically built into the walls of our house. I roll over in bed, turning my face away from the too-bright window. I'm surprised to be waking up when it felt like I'd never fall asleep last night. Exhaustion still has a hold on me, and I close my eyes, trying to squeeze out another hour of sleep before I have to wake up and face yet another day of not knowing what to do.

I grab my fluffy down comforter and pull it up to my face, willing the sleep to come back to me. Sleep is the only time I'm not stressing about Luca and college. Sweet, perfect, sleep.

The voices from downstairs get louder. I hear my mom say, "She's still asleep but go wake her up."

I freeze. *Why is he here?*

Luca's athletic footsteps are never soft on the stairs, and I can hear him approaching from the moment he walks out of the kitchen. I close my eyes, squeezing the comforter close, hoping like hell that I look asleep right now. Maybe he'll see me sleeping and leave.

A soft tap sounds on my door and I panic for a moment, thinking maybe it's not Luca but someone else. Luca doesn't knock. He just walks right on in, usually diving onto my bed to be as annoying as possible when he wakes me up. Sometimes he even makes this god-awful crowing rooster sound.

But I smell his body wash a few seconds later and know for sure that it's him. I keep my eyes closed as he walks around my bed. *Please just go away.*

The bed sinks down in the middle as Luca sits on it. Then he lays down, the air carrying the scent of him, all clean and fresh out of the shower. I love that body wash. I picked it out the last time we were at Target. My heart pangs with the memory of the two of us, goofing off, our shopping cart overflowing with crap we didn't really need. That was just a few months ago. Back when I hadn't yet been accepted to FLU and we weren't falling apart at the seams.

Luca inhales deeply. I chance opening my eyes and I see him lying next to me, his hands folded together over his stomach, his eyes on the ceiling. He doesn't look over, but he must sense that I'm awake.

"I hate this, babe."

"I hate it, too," I mumble, the comforter still wrapped tightly around me. A literal security blanket.

He keeps his gaze to the ceiling. "This was the worst week of my life. I'm so sorry for how I acted."

"I'm sorry, too."

He turns to look at me. "Everyone is just going on like normal. Our parents. Our friends. Everything is so fine for everyone else but I'm over here falling apart. I don't know what to do."

"I should have never applied to FLU," I say.

"No, Honey." He shakes his head. "No... I want you to be happy and if that school will make you happy then..." His head turns back and he looks at the ceiling again. "I want you to be happy."

I push the comforter down. "Really? Are you really saying you support me going away to college?"

"I—" Luca's jaw works and then he closes it. "Yes, I want you to be happy but... But I can't sit here and act like your happiness won't completely ruin me, because it will."

Disappointment crashes back into me as quickly as it had left.

I roll my eyes so hard it sends a sharp pain through my skull. "Then can we just drop it?"

Luca's hand covers mine, his fingers wrapping around my palm. "Yes. Let's just drop it. I love you, babe. I don't want to fight with my soulmate."

I sit up in my bed, taking his hands in both of mine. The rough callouses on his palms are softer than usual. They always heal over during track season when he works less construction than he does in the summer. When I lift my eyes, I find him looking at me, a curious gaze peering back at me.

"Luca... are we soulmates?"

His lips slide into a frown, his eyebrows following quickly after. "Why wouldn't we be soulmates?"

I swallow, last night's research study fresh in my mind. All of this might have come up because of the college thing, but I've been wondering about Luca and me for months now. That awful, nagging bit of doubt has been clinging to me, whispering in my ear. Every time a friend gets asked on a date by a cute new guy. Every time someone gets doe-eyed and flushed when talking about their first kiss. Giggling over getting a college guy's number at a beach party.

All those little things that come with dating and falling in love and finding the right person for you—I didn't get any of that. If Luca and I stay together forever, I'll never know what it's like to meet someone and fall in love. Luca and I have just always *been*. We've never *started*.

My best friend Maggie's riveting tales of the brief summer

fling she had last year had nearly been my undoing. All that talk of heart-pounding, toe-tingling feelings was hard to endure. Instead of being happy for her, I was just envious. I don't remember the last time my heart pounded around Luca. Or if it ever has.

Luca sits up. There's not much space between us on my queen-sized bed, but we feel farther apart than ever. I watch his chest rise and fall while he watches me, waiting for an answer.

"*Are* we soulmates?" I ask, my voice soft.

"Yes." He exhales sharply. "Yes, Honey. We are. I know it, you know it, the whole damn town knows it."

"No, the town knows that we have these adorable parents with an adorable love story and they pushed us into the same story, wanting us to be just like them."

Luca flinches like I've just punched him in the face. "And you don't want that for us? You don't want the happy ending, perfect love story that our parents have?"

"Of course I do."

"So why are you saying we aren't soulmates?"

"Well…" I shrug. "We didn't choose each other, Luca. We've just always known each other. We've been together every day since we were born."

I can't believe how good it feels to say that out loud, even if it is making Luca stare at me like he doesn't even know who I am anymore.

Luca looks down, his hands bunching the sheets tightly. "What will it take to prove to you that we're soulmates?"

I motion to the nightstand next to him. "Will you get my laptop?"

He hands it over to me and I open it. The screen flickers to life, revealing the same webpage I was on last night. I realize my heart is pounding, but not in the falling-in-love way. I hand it back to him. "I found this last night."

Luca frowns but he starts to read. I sit here, watching his eyes go back and forth as he takes in the same article that had felt so life-changing to me last night. A few minutes later, he reaches the end, and then looks up at me. He doesn't look like he's had the same revelation I had.

"You think that because we haven't dated anyone else we can't be soulmates?"

"Not that we can't be soulmates..." I say, my voice rising in a way that makes it sound like a question. "Just that... well... we might not be. I don't want to go our whole lives thinking we're in love when really, maybe ... we're not."

Saying those last words feels like pushing a two-ton boulder uphill. But I said it, and now it's out there, and even if this blows up in my face, at least I spoke what was on my heart.

Luca watches me for a long moment, his eyes flitting across my face, taking it all in, I guess. This past week. The article he just read. My surprising college confession.

He reaches for my hand, his thumb sliding across my knuckles. "I love you so much, Honey. I always have and... I always will."

His other hand reaches up to touch my cheek. My eyes close, and I breathe in the scent of him. The comforting feel of his hand on my skin. I love Luca. That part isn't up for debate. But that doesn't change the feeling of the crack in my heart, that black sliver of doubt that won't go away.

"Let's do it," Luca says, dropping his hand. "Let's split up —*temporarily*—" he adds when my eyes go wide. "Instead of five relationships, let's go on five dates. And if, at the end of it, you still think we're not soulmates, then fine. We can break up and you can go to your college and it just… is what it is, I guess."

"Are you serious?" I ask.

He nods. "I think so."

I can't help but laugh. "This is a pretty big deal."

"Yeah, but *we* are a big deal, Honey. I don't want you to go your whole life wondering if we're soulmates. I want you to know it for sure."

He pulls his phone from his pocket and opens it to the calendar app. "There are five weeks left of school, so it works out perfectly. We'll go on five dates over the next five weeks. And then by graduation, you can tell me if we're getting back together or not."

"Why is it up to me?" I ask. "You might find your real soulmate out there."

He shakes his head without giving it a single split second of thought. "You're my soulmate. But—if you want incontrovertible proof that we're perfect together, then I can do this for you."

My breathing feels shallow as I take in what he just said. This idea… it's crazy and wild and it might actually work. I know I love Luca. But I also know I want more. I peer up at him. "Five dates," I say.

"Five dates."

Even though it's completely hypocritical of me, the idea of someone else with their tongue down his throat makes me want to scream. "One more thing… no kissing."

"No kissing?"

I'm not sure if he's asking or just repeating what I said.

I nod. "I mean, it's just first dates, not long term relationships… we shouldn't kiss any of them, right?"

"How do you know you're in love if you can't kiss someone?"

My objection comes out in a huff of air. "You want to kiss other girls?"

The way he stares blankly at me, offering nothing but a stupid shrug, makes me want to call off the whole thing. Here I am freaking out about the success and happiness of my entire future, *at great personal stress I might add*, and he's over here seeing this as an opportunity to make out with new people?

My arms fold over my chest. "Are you serious right now?"

"I'm not saying I'm going to jog out of your house and make out with the first girl I see. I'm just saying if it happens, it happens."

My nostrils flare.

"Babe, it's a compromise," he says. "That's what all the experts say good relationships have. Compromise."

I close my eyes and picture my dream college. I visualize myself waking up in a dorm at FLU, a happy, independent woman. That woman, the woman I want to be, wouldn't obsess over this kissing thing.

Unfortunately, I'm not her yet.

"You're an ass."

"We're still going to be friends, right? I don't want to spend the next five weeks ignoring each other." Those deep blue eyes turn their puppy look on me and I crumble.

"No way, we're still friends," I say, touching his arm. "We're always friends."

"Good. Let's get breakfast," Luca says, standing up. "I was so depressed I could barely eat all week, but now I'm starving."

"You're taking this pretty well," I say, eyeing him suspiciously as I get up and let the covers crumple back over my bed. My bed gets made about once a year, and it's not going to be today.

"Eh, I'm not worried." He shrugs one shoulder and leans over, kissing the top of my head. "We'll find our way back to each other. That's what soulmates do."

"Luca?" I say over the lump that just formed in my throat. "If we're really going to do this…we should probably tell our parents."

CHAPTER FIVE

A lump has formed in my throat at some point in the last ten minutes and I'm pretty sure it'll stay here forever, partially blocking my airway and making my chest feel tight until I die of old age.

"This is going to ruin Saturday morning waffles…" I mutter as we venture out my back door and across backyards toward Luca's house.

"Nothing can ruin waffles," Luca says, tossing me an upbeat little side grin.

"We're about to tell our parents we're breaking up. It'll crush them."

"*Temporarily* breaking up," he says.

"Temporarily but maybe permanently," I say.

"Maybe permanently but maybe temporarily." Luca's eyebrow's wiggle as he flings open his back door with a dramatic flourish.

The door leads into the kitchen which smells like maple syrup, coffee, and melted butter—a Saturday tradition. It's usually the greatest smell ever, but today it turns my stomach.

"Moms and Dads," Luca says, keeping up with the dramatic door opening. It's like he's some theater kid instead of an athlete— "Honey and I just decided to break up."

I expect everything to go silent. Maybe some jaw-dropping. Or my mom rushing over and throwing her arms around me to comfort me in this time of great tragedy. Despite my boyfriend's dramatics (well, ex-boyfriend, I guess), the parents just look over at us. Jill cocks an eyebrow, one hand on her waffle iron. The dads, sitting next to each other across the kitchen island, exchange the smallest of confused glances. Mom clears her throat, but she stays sitting on the barstool. She doesn't even attempt to hug me. "Well, this is unexpected."

"It's an experiment," Luca says, putting an arm around my shoulders. "We're breaking up and dating five different people just to see if we're actually soulmates or not. If we are, we'll get back together after graduation."

"I got the idea from Google," I add, glancing at my mom. She told me to Google my problem, after all. The corners of her lips quirk for just a second before her face turns passive and she looks over at Dad.

"Ah, so it's some social media challenge thing?" Dad says, not looking at Mom. But they've been married so long I'm sure he knows what she's thinking anyhow.

"It's not a social media thing. It's real life," I say, biting back my annoyance. We just delivered pretty big news and they don't even care. Luca's arm falls from around my shoulders and he takes one of the two remaining plates on the kitchen island.

"Wow. Broken up?" Jill says with nothing but a bit of humor in her voice, because apparently no one realizes this is a big deal. "So you'll find five other people to date?"

"Just one date each," Luca says. He takes a waffle from the pile next to the waffle maker, bites into it, then drops it on the plate to cover in syrup. "It's an experiment. Then we get back together."

I press my tongue into my teeth.

Luca's dad, Tony, chuckles. "I feel bad for the poor souls who think they can separate you two."

"For sure," Jill says, lifting the iron and sliding the golden waffle onto the last plate, which she holds out to me. "You kids are the real deal."

Dad nods over his cup of coffee. "No one else stands a chance."

Mom is silent as she reaches for the bottle of maple syrup, but her silence might as well be agreement with the others. Why does everyone think Luca and I will be together forever? If we are such perfect soulmates, why am I the only one not convinced?

———

I borrow Moms' car and head straight to Maggie's around two in the afternoon when she should be finishing up her weekly makeup video. She typically spends all morning filming, then all afternoon editing. With any luck, her persistence will pay off and she'll finally get more subscribers than Makeup Maria, who is her MUA YouTuber rival. They've both been accepted into a badass cosmetology school in NYC, and while they haven't met in real life, or even mentioned each other in their videos, it's obvious they are in competition, constantly trying to one-up each other.

I park in front of the third car garage slot just off to the right of Maggie's grandiose white brick house. Maggie lives in

Bridgeland, Stonebrook's newest subdivision, which features the town's nicest homes. Mom loves when she gets a new listing here because the commission can pay the bills for months.

The front door swings open before I knock. Mr. Sinclair smiles at me with a pencil between his teeth. "Come on in," he mumbles—at least I think that's what he says over the pencil—"Maggie's upstairs."

The living room furniture has been pushed aside to make room for Mr. Sinclair's newest architectural model. Made with thin wood, sheets of plastic for windows, and silver metal bits, this miniature hotel thingy on the coffee table looks luxurious. I lean down to admire it. He even has little plastic people glued to the fake sidewalks, and tiny plastic trees for scenery. A blue water fountain with some kind of resin water proudly decorates the entrance.

"Where is this being built?" I ask.

Mr. Sinclair slides the pencil into his front shirt pocket then frowns down at his creation. "Vegas. Hopefully. Still need to win the bid."

His voice is deep and serious, but the English accent is just like Maggie's, and the way he furrows his brows reminds me of her, too. Of course, I know better than to say that because the last time I compared my best friend to her towering, dark-skinned father, she got upset. Apparently Maggie shares a jawline with her dad instead of her mom and as a makeup artist, that is a very, very bad thing.

I wish him good luck on his bid and then I jog upstairs to Maggie's bedroom. Her door is closed and the handmade "leave me alone, I'm recording" sign is hanging from the door-knob. I send her a text letting her know I'm here.

A few moments later, the door opens.

I burst into tears.

"Holy shite," Maggie says. "Does my makeup look that bad?"

It's an exaggerated cat eyeliner thing with pink shimmery eyeshadow. It doesn't look bad at all; it looks amazing. I shake my head.

"What's wrong?" She ushers me to her bed and I blink away the tears. When blinking doesn't stop them, I press my fingers to the corners of my eyes. I didn't cry when Luca and I agreed to break up. I didn't cry when we told the parents. Why am I crying now?"

I take a deep breath, inhaling until my lungs burn, and then I let it all out. "Luca and I broke up."

Maggie blinks. "Huh?"

This makes me laugh. "We broke up."

"Wow." My usually chatty best friend has been reduced to one word responses. I know I should tell her about the whole five dates thing, but right now I just need someone to believe me. Someone to think we are broken up and not tell me I'm crazy for it.

"Say something more than that," I urge her.

Maggie's glossy lips press together. "You and Luca are the perfect couple. This is… so weird."

"I *hate* that word," I say, turning away. "We are not perfect."

"Since when?"

I look at Maggie and realize I forgot to ask Shawn Beck if he's dating anyone, like I'd promised her I'd do last week. Part of me wants to start talking about that, change the subject to something easy. But maybe the topic of boys isn't so easy anymore.

"Since I got accepted into FLU."

A look of realization settles over her face. "Luca doesn't want you to go."

I nod. "I told him I got accepted and he got mad and I got mad and we fought and..." I take a deep breath. "I don't want to give up my dream college. I don't want to give up my boyfriend. But..." My teeth dig into my lip. "Actually... it's not just the college thing."

Maggie's brows lift.

It feels weird admitting this, but I have to say it. "I'm not sure Luca is my soulmate. And I can't just spend my whole life wondering... so... we're doing an experiment." I tell her about the five dates thing and the scientific study I found. Then I tell her now no one seems to take this seriously—not Luca, not our parents. She watches me with eyes so wide I'm not sure they'll ever go back to their normal size.

"This is a problem for chocolate." Maggie stands and reaches for my hand. "We need chocolate."

Mrs. Sinclair is a professional baker. Wedding cakes are her specialty, and she's booked months in advance. Today she's delivering a cake that's so large it takes two delivery vans to transport it.

I'm pretty sure it's the best profession you could ask for from your friend's parents. The Sinclair's pantry is always stocked with freshly baked deliciousness. Down in the kitchen, Maggie loads up a plate with chocolate cupcakes, cookies, mini strawberry tarts, and a handful of chocolate chips and from her mom's ingredient shelf in the pantry.

We take our sugary smorgasbord upstairs to her bedroom, bypassing her dad who is still working on his architectural model while watching soccer on the TV. Luckily he doesn't ask what we're up to—I'm not sure I can deal with telling more people about the break up just yet.

Maggie's decorating style is clean and simple, with white wooden furniture and teal accents. I love it. My room is filled with keepsakes and random crap from my childhood since I've lived there my whole life. Every time I want to clean it out, I can't bear to part with my old toys and junk. Maggie didn't have that problem because they put most of their stuff in storage before moving abroad.

Maggie sits on her bed, the tray of food in between us. She leans forward, her eyes sparkling pools of curiosity. "Do you think this five dates plan will work? Or is it just..." She wobbles her hand in the air. "Is it just the calm before the storm?"

I reach for a piece of peppermint bark and bite down on it to buy myself a few more seconds to answer.

"I don't think so. I don't know."

"You don't know, or you don't think so?" she asks.

"I—" I close my mouth. The lump in my throat that's been there all week seems to triple in size. "I don't want to break up, but I kind of do want to break up. If it's not college, it'll be something else. There's always something else we disagree about. We aren't like our parents. The moms and dads get along really well, but Luca and I are always fighting about something stupid."

She runs her finger over the whipped buttercream icing of the cupcake in front of her and licks it off. "Do you really think you'll meet your real soulmate before graduation?"

I snort. "I'm not sure I'll meet five whole people to date, much less a friggen soulmate." I don't realize I'm biting my lip until I taste blood. Then a whole new horror comes to mind. "What is everyone at school going to say?" I sink my head into my hands. "I can't face them tomorrow."

"Yes you can," Maggie says. "Stay over at my house tonight

and I'll drive us to school tomorrow. It'll be like ripping off a bandage when you show up without him."

I reach for a piece of chocolate. "That's a good idea."

Maggie's eyes crinkle in the corners, her perfectly shaped brows pulling together. "You'll be fine, I promise. We just need to find you date number one," she says, her English accent more pronounced as she gazes down at the tray of junk food before choosing a single white chocolate chip. "And you're in luck."

"Why's that?" I say with a snort. "Are you going to do my makeup for me?"

"Well, obvs." She tips her head back and scoops a handful of white chocolate chips into her mouth. "But the real lucky part here," she mumbles over the chocolate, "is that I am a perfect wing woman."

CHAPTER SIX

Several years ago the parents decided that age twelve was the official age they'd let Luca and me get cell phones. Luca's birthday is two months before mine, and although his parents got him the newest model iPhone and it was pretty freaking cool, his phone sat untouched on his nightstand until I got mine two months later. From that day forward, Luca and I were always just one house, one bedroom window, and one phone call apart from each other.

Every night he texts me:

Goodnight. I love you.

And every night I text back:

Goodnight. I love you more.

Sometimes the words change a bit. Or they'll be mistakenly misspelled. Or I'll toss in an emoji, or Luca will shorten Goodnight to "gn", but no matter what, Luca has texted me goodnight every single day since my twelfth birthday. He even does it when I fall asleep on his couch and end up spending the night next to him. It's our little ritual, one of those parts of our relationship that make my friends jealous.

He didn't text me last night.

I would have known the second he did text—if he did—because I didn't sleep all night. Maggie's bed is comfortable and all, but it was like the second the lights went out, all I could think about was freedom and heartbreak and college and the ridiculous idea that I will be dating five other people. It's exciting and terrifying.

Maggie is trying to act cool about it all, but I'm pretty sure she's just as weirded out as I am when we drive to school the next morning. Without saying anything, she parks on the opposite side of the school parking lot. It's her little way of acknowledging how awkward it would be if she parked right next to Luca's truck like usual. Normally she waits for us to arrive in Luca's truck and the three of us walk into school together. This is just one of the millions of little changes that are going to happen now that we're broken up.

Or maybe we'll get back together and everything will go back to normal.

In the row ahead of us, a sophomore struggles to pull her large tuba case from the backseat of her car. I watch her, how she pulls and shoves, sweating in the morning humidity, trying to make something work when it's clearly not meant to. I try not to draw comparisons of a stupid tuba to my relationship.

Maggie puts her car in park and turns to me with a big, YouTube star smile. "You ready?"

I blow a raspberry with my tongue.

"Come on. I'll buy you a coffee."

The morning air feels like lead in my lungs. I grip my backpack straps as we walk toward Stonebrook High.

"You look like somebody died," Maggie says, side eyeing

me. "Chin up. You're a single woman now, and you're in the market for a hot date."

I groan. "People will want details. Everyone will talk about it. I have no idea what to say."

"You two didn't organize some way to reveal the breakup to everyone?" Maggie asks, holding the door open for me.

"What, like we're celebrities?" I snort. "No, we didn't type up a note saying we've decided to break up and please respect our privacy at this difficult time."

"Maybe you should have," she says. "You two *are* small town celebrities."

"Whoa, whoa, whoa." The deep voice comes from my left. It's Tyler Markson. He was on the track team for about five seconds this year before he got kicked off for vaping THC in math class. I don't know where he came from but suddenly he's walking right next to me. "You and Luca broke up?"

I roll my eyes. "I like how you can't pay attention to our group chemistry project but you can pay attention to conversations that have nothing to do with you."

He smirks. "This is more interesting than chemistry."

"Piss off," Maggie says. Coming from anyone else that might sound rude, but in her melodic voice, it's not nearly as insulting. "She's too good for you."

Tyler holds up his hands. "No worries. I'm not making a move. Luca would kill me."

Maggie and I get iced coffee from the cafeteria and then she waits with me in my first period class until the bell rings. Things feel normal for all of ten seconds. Mrs. Wallace hasn't even finished going over the warm up before I feel someone's eyes on me. I glance over.

Jaxon nods at me. It's just a simple jerk of his head, but I know he knows I'm single now. It's weird getting attention from guys, but it's even weirder knowing I can just go on a date with someone if I want. But not Jaxon. He has the maturity of a toddler, plus I'm ninety-nine percent sure he's dating a freshman. I look back at my notebook.

As soon as Mrs. Wallace's lesson is over, Jaycee turns around in her chair and faces me with wide eyes. "Is it true?" she whispers.

I nod. Her eyes get even bigger. "What happened?"

I shrug. "It's…" I have to stop myself from saying *temporary*. "… mutual."

Jaycee's expression says she doesn't believe that for one second. "Seriously," I say. "We're still friends. We might even get back together… I don't know."

"Oh," she says softly. "Okay." She turns back around.

She's doing a really bad job of hiding her disappointment for someone who has been my casual friend since third grade. My phone buzzes from my back pocket.

> **Luca:** Holy crap. Everyone knows.
> **Me:** I know.
> **Luca:** It's weird.
> **Me:** yup.

I watch the phone screen until the bell rings, staring at the text I haven't sent yet. *I miss you.* Luca hasn't texted me again, so there's no reason to send it. Plus… I'm not entirely sure I do miss him. I think I might just miss our routine; the comfort of going to school without being the center of attention.

It's Monday, which is STEM Club day. Tomorrow I will have to brave the cafeteria without Luca, but today I get to hide out at lunch with my favorite group of nerds. We meet once a week in an empty science lab. I love my nerd friends. Besides Maggie, all of my normal friends are just Luca's athlete friends. But these people represent a different side of me. We formed the STEM Club in eighth grade, and it's been just the five of us ever since. We've tried the occasional campaign to recruit more members, but no one takes notice of our hand painted signs in the hallways. It doesn't matter how small we are; my nerd friends are the only people besides Aunt Bree who will be excited that I was accepted into Fault Line University.

I haven't exactly told them yet. Until I know for sure if I'm actually going to FLU, I don't want anyone else to know. Mason was recently accepted to FLU and it's all he talks about. Our fearless STEM Club president, Janise, is going to MIT next year. Anna got into UCLA. When our conversations turn to colleges, I always sit back and let them talk.

Today we're discussing the upcoming Youth STEM Conference in Houston. As I make my way toward the science lab, I pull up the hotel info on my phone. They'll be psyched that I was able to secure discount pricing for our two rooms, and that as long as we have an adult's name on the paperwork, the hotel won't care if we're unsupervised.

All eyes are on me when I walk into the science lab. I don't think anyone cares about hotel rates right now. Well, all eyes except for Mason's. He's kneeling on the floor with his head under the table. He absolutely refuses to let it go that one of the table legs wobbles no matter what he does to try to fix it.

I drop my lunch bag on the table. "You all have sixty seconds to ask whatever you want to ask and then we are *so* not talking about this anymore."

"So it's true?" Janise says. She's always had pink in her dreadlocks, but now the pink has been replaced with cardinal red, an homage to MIT. She tosses the locks over her shoulder. "You and Luca actually broke up?"

I take a deep breath. "Yeah… so, here's the deal. I got accepted into FLU."

"WHAT! Honey! Ohmygod!" Anna claps her hands together under her chin, her blue eyes sparkling beneath tons of black eyeliner. "That's an awesome college!"

I grin. It feels really good to tell someone, to pretend that maybe, just maybe, I'll go to my dream school. "I told Luca about FLU and … we decided to break up.."

Mason's dark eyes peer up at me from just above the table. I'm not in the mood to deal with him, so I look at rest of the group, all scattered around the front two tables in the classroom with their lunches.

"Wow," Janise breathes. "You've been dating forever. Are you okay?"

I nod and pop open the top to my can of sparkling water. "I'm fine."

Vu clears his throat from across the table. He's a year younger than the rest of us. It's not uncommon for him to go all meeting without saying a word. He's cool, though. Smart and efficient, and top of his class. "I heard about the five dates experiment. What academic journal published it?"

"Wait, what?" Janise says, pushing away her lunch and leaning forward. "We need details on whatever this is."

"How do you know about that?" I ask.

Vu shrugs. "I heard Luca talking about it last period."

My cheeks burn. The five dates experiment sounds like a great idea when it's just Luca and me who know about it. But the rest of the school? My STEM Club? This is mortifying.

Vu continues, either not noticing or not caring that I'm probably ten shades of pink right now. "There's a study online which concluded that people find their soulmate after five relationships. Luca said you two are going to go on five dates and then deciding if you're getting back together or not. I think it's fascinating. We need more academic studies on human relationships."

"That is so cool," Janise says, turning to a new page in her notebook. "Let's make this our next project. We'll help you track the dates and compile stats, and maybe we can get other couples on board—"

"No," I say.

"It could be fun," Anna says. "I'm game for dating five girls and seeing if it leads to my soulmate."

"Then you can be the guinea pig," I say. "Leave me out of it."

"Noooo," Anna says, pushing out her bottom lip. "We should all do it. We're all single, right? It'll be fun. Dating in the name of science."

"I'm not dating anyone until after grad school," Janise says.

"How are you supposed to find these dates?" Vu asks me. "Do you ask guys out or do you wait for them to come to you? I wonder if that would have an effect on the results."

Mason stands up, brushing his long-ish black hair out of his face. "Clearly Honey's love life is of the upmost importance in a STEM Club, so I'm really glad that we're wasting so much time talking about it."

"I can't believe I'm agreeing with Mason, but I agree with Mason," I say. "Let's move on. I have updates on our conference hotel."

"Ugh, you guys are no fun," Anna says, crossing her arms over her chest. "This will help you get over your breakup, Honey."

"I don't need help getting over it."

"Science. Technology. Engineering. Math." Mason holds up four fingers, one for each word. "There is no *dating* in STEM Club."

"Technically, it would fall under Science," Vu says.

Mason exhales. "If you all want to proceed with something this asinine, I'm excluding myself." His eyes slide to me. "I can't believe I'm agreeing with Honey, but I agree with Honey."

I grin. He's unbearable but he's useful sometimes. Without him, I wouldn't be such a skilled trash talker. Mason is the kind of person who thinks he's extremely smart. And he is. But the fact that he knows he's smart makes him insufferable. We've been mortal enemies for as long as I can remember. But we're the kind of enemies who put up with each other out of a love of science.

"It's been way longer than sixty seconds," I say, checking the time on my phone. "Can we please change the subject? The whole school is talking about me and I just need a few minutes with friends who won't talk about it. Please."

"Of course." Janise flips to another page in her notebook and begins the meeting by going over the upcoming conference schedule.

I stare at my uneaten lunch, knowing I'll be hungry later if I don't eat but I can't seem to make myself hungry right now. While Janise talks, I can feel Mason's eyes on me. When I glance at him he looks away. Knowing him, he's already concocted a billion snappy insults about my newfound single girl status.

At least he's smart enough to keep them to himself.

CHAPTER SEVEN

The loud, tinny screech of a T-Rex fills the air as soon as I open the car door. Maggie jumps, covering her ears and scowling up at the life-sized concrete replica of everyone's favorite short-armed dinosaur.

"I should have dictated more rules for this boy-finding event," she mutters as she slings the thin strap of her handbag across her body. "No annoying dinosaurs would have been the first rule."

I walk around the car and link my arm through hers. "True love doesn't follow rules."

I'm not sure I believe that, but it's the first thing to come to my mind. When Maggie insisted on going out after school to find my first date, I immediately thought of my favorite place. Dinosaur Valley.

State parks don't exactly scream: "find your soulmate here!" Especially on a Tuesday afternoon when the parking lot has all of three cars in it. I know the soulmate clock is ticking —I have less than two months to go on five dates—but I'm in over my head here. I have no idea how to find a guy and flirt and convince him to ask me on a date. Something tells me it won't be as easy as it is in the movies.

A shudder zaps through my body. I am so not cut out for this.

We stop at the gate and I scan my park membership card which allows me one free guest. I ignore Maggie's jabs about how I'm as dorky as an old cat lady for having a lifetime membership card to a dinosaur-themed state park.

Stonebrook is a small country town with one shopping mall and two boring parks. Dinosaur Valley is the closest escape you can find in this part of Texas. Here, you can close your eyes and be one with nature. You can sit under a tree or on a rock ledge and read a book all day, or study, or just chill out. My earliest childhood memories all involve coming to Dinosaur Valley with my parents and Luca's family, having picnics with Lunchables and juice boxes, and splashing around in the legendary Paluxy River.

The park is popular on the weekends, but it's is mostly empty today. An older man walks three dogs on long leashes and a young mother sits on a park bench, watching her kids splash their feet in the river.

"How exactly are we supposed to find hot guys for you to date when there are no guys here at all?" Maggie says, squishing her face into a frown. "I'm beginning to think you brought me here because you *don't* want to find your soulmate."

"No way. This is a hot guy breeding ground. Plus, any guy who comes to the park is probably interested in the geosciences, so he's more likely to be my soulmate than some loser hanging out at the mall."

The mall had been Maggie's idea of a place to find my first date. I shot that idea down quickly, because, *ew*. If I really am going to find my soulmate on one of these dates, it won't be at the lame-o Stonebrook Mall. I am not going to gather my future grandchildren around the Christmas tree one day and tell them the story of how I met their grandfather in front of the Lady Foot Locker. When I meet my real soulmate—assuming it's not Luca—it's going to be somewhere romantic. It'll be a story worth telling.

I lead us straight to the river, which is the second best attraction of the park, right after the long hiking trails that take you way up the hillside, giving you a view of the beautiful west Texas landscape. I've been wanting to take Maggie ever since she moved here, and it's kind of a shame that it took breaking up with my boyfriend to finally make that happen.

"Are these real dinosaur footprints?" Maggie asks, peering over her sunglasses as we approach the riverbed. "I find that hard to believe. They'd have to be, like, millions of years old."

"A hundred and twelve million years old," I say.

When the water is clear, like today when the park is mostly empty without kids aren't splashing around in the river, you can see right to the bottom. Ancient dinosaur tracks are preserved in the riverbed from where the majestic creatures used to roam around before whatever meteoroid or alien intervention came and wiped them out.

"Those are sauropod tracks," I say, pointing to the scattered fossilized footprints in front of us. I kick off my sandals and bend down, rolling up my jeans until they reach my knees. I step into the warm water. "Come on, it's only a few inches deep."

Maggie looks scandalized at the idea of taking off her black leather heels, but she does, shoving them in her purse for safekeeping. She's wearing a champagne colored dress that goes to her knees, so although she's overdressed for school like always, she's perfectly dressed for a random walk through the river. The water doesn't get any deeper than our knees.

"They don't look like dinosaur tracks," she says, casting a scrutinizing look at the roundish, elephant-shaped indentions in the riverbed below.

Maggie pokes her toes at the fossilized footprint in front of her. I step into one. Both of my feet fit inside one print. "If we walk a little further down, there's Allosaurus tracks. They have three toes and look like more of what you'd expect for a dinosaur."

"You mean Acrocanthosaurus tracks."

I turn around, startled to hear a familiar voice behind me. Mason stands in the water, his black jeans rolled up to his calves. He gives me a crooked grin that disappears quickly, almost like he regrets talking.

"I know what I meant," I bite out, slapping a hand on my hip.

He lowers his hand, resting it on the clunky digital camera that hangs from a strap around his neck. "Sorry... I didn't mean to eavesdrop."

"And yet you did." I am not about to let him correct my knowledge of dinosaurs at my favorite state park.

Mason smirks, dragging a foot through the water as he steps closer. "The Allosaurus is still a theropod, but it's not what made these tracks. They weighed around, eh, three thousand pounds give or take. Not nearly heavy enough to make these deep impressions. The Acrocanthosaurus weighed almost seven tons." He points to the fossilized footprints below us. "That's what made this."

My nostrils flare. The only thing worse than arguing with Mason while standing in a river with my jeans tugged up to my knees and my leg hairs in need of a razor is realizing that he's is correct. I know it's the Acrocanthosaurus. Of course I know that. Why did I say Allosaurus? Am I just so screwed up from this breakup and dating thing that I can't keep my dinosaur species sorted out in my head?

The last thing I want to do is admit that he's corrected me on my own home turf—my favorite place in the world, the state park I wrote about in my application essay to FLU—but he's right and he knows he's right.

I shrug. "Yeah, that's what I meant. Acrocanthosaurus."

"Don't mind me," Maggie says, kicking her foot through the warm water. "It's not like I'm over here memorizing dinosaur names. After all," she says, giving me a very knowing look—the kind of look you don't need to be her best friend to understand—"That's not why we came here today."

I flash a look right back at her and then start walking. "Come on, I'll show you my favorite set of tracks. Maybe Mason can follow us and try to correct everything I say."

"Wait," Maggie says, turning toward our uninvited guest. "Hi, I'm Maggie." She holds out her hand to my nerdy, annoying, mortal enemy who totally needs a haircut. "You two already know each other?"

"We're in STEM Club together."

Recognition flashes in her eyes. "Oooh, right. Mason the annoying STEM Club guy," she says. "You look much different than I pictured."

"You talk about me?" Mason asks, tilting to see me past Maggie.

I roll my eyes. "I *complain* about you."

He grins. "I guess Honey describes me as some devil with horns instead of a short Filipino guy?"

Maggie nods. "Something like that."

"We're going now." I start walking but Maggie stays standing in her fossilized footprint.

"You a journalism student?" she asks, pointing to the camera around Mason's neck. The lanyard is printed with Property of Stonebrook High.

He shakes his head. "Nah, I'm just getting some photos of my favorite places to take with me to college in the fall."

"Very cool," Maggie says. "Are you going to that conference thing with Honey?"

"Yep."

"You can go back to taking pictures now." I flash him a quick, tight-lipped smile, then grab my best friend's hand. "Let's go."

We walk all the way to the bend in the river before I speak again. "Why did you keep talking to him? He's the worst."

Maggie grins. "You should ask that boy out."

"Oh, hell no." I stick out my tongue and shudder. "Did you see the way he acted? All *'hi, I'm so much smarter than you, let me brag on my smartness like some kind of jackass'*…"

Maggie laughs so hard it echoes off the water. "Oh come on. You talk about him all the time."

"I *do not* talk about him all the time!"

"Yes, you do!"

"Only on days after STEM Club, because he's annoying and I hate him."

"He's cute though."

"Who cares."

"So you admit he's cute?"

I roll my eyes. "I'm *so* not digging this inquisition right now, Mags."

That only makes her laugh again.

"You're totally wrong about this." I stop in front of an

Acrocanthosaurus track and turn to her, shielding the sun from my eyes with the back of my hand. "Mason and I have a mutual hatred of each other. My five dates need to be with someone I actually like being around or the experiment will be flawed."

"Fine," she drawls, holding up her hands in surrender. "My face is about to melt off in this heat. Let's go find cute guys in a building with air conditioning."

CHAPTER EIGHT

The R&B box van is huge and clunky and drives like a school bus. It has two large fake leather seats up front that make you sit so high you feel like your feet won't be able to touch the floor, and the back is all open space for hauling furniture. The parents wanted something useful, not pretty, when they purchased this thing a couple of years ago. Aunt Bree's friend runs a vinyl graphic shop and they gave us a great discount on the custom R&B logo decals on each side of the van.

The decals look nice, but the rest of this thing sucks. And I'm the one who always seems to get stuck driving it. I can feel the other drivers' annoyance with me as I crawl to a stop at each red light and then slowly chug, chug, chug forward, clunkily shifting gears with all the expertise of someone who doesn't drive stick shift regularly.

The only good thing about these excursions is that sometimes I get to pick out the furniture. We're partnered with Shoreline Furniture, another family-owned business two towns over. Their massive showroom is located in an old Walmart building. The dads arranged a furniture rental contract where we get a cheap price to rent discontinued furniture to stage the homes we have for sale. The moms stage living rooms, bedrooms, and game rooms in a pleasing way so that potential home buyers will be more likely to buy the house. Shoreline Furniture then offers the homebuyer a huge discount if they choose to buy the furniture when they buy the house.

Unfortunately, the last house we sold was to someone who had their own furniture. So it's all going back. I drive around the back of the store and then park next to the unloading dock. Jill wants me to rent outdoor furniture for a new listing that has a patio almost as big as the house itself. The only instructions she gave me were "colorful and modern", which means I get to choose the specific pieces. This is one part of the job I really love. It's not the world-changing stuff geophysicists do, but it's fun.

I climb down from the van and brush off my palms on my denim shorts. I always get a little sweaty and nervous when driving this stupid thing. A guy in a tan Shoreline polo shirt walks out of the big bay door.

"Hello," he says, flashing me a bright smile. I know that smile—it's the customer service smile, one you have to put on when you're on the clock even though you couldn't care less about whoever you're talking to. This guy looks about my age, maybe a little bit older. He's Hispanic, with short dark hair, tanned skin and broad shoulders. His left arm is covered in intricate, colorful tattoos.

"Hi," I say. "I'm here for Marco."

"Marco's not here. Emergency gall bladder surgery."

I grimace. "Is he okay?"

The guy nods. "He'll be all right, but I'm filling in for him until he gets back. I'm Josh. What can I do for you?"

I smack my hand on the van's back door. "I'm returning this stuff and renting some patio furniture."

"Cool," he says, pressing his palms together in front of his chest. It makes his biceps ripple, and it's hard to look away. I guess moving furniture all day gets you in shape. "Let's get started."

I unlock the back doors and Josh helps me carry out the black leather loveseat. We shuffle up the ramp at the back of the store and then set it down next to a few other couches. This part of the store is all rental and discount furniture, and it's organized by type.

"You're pretty strong," Josh says, flashing me a sincere grin as we walk back through the large warehouse door into the bright sunshine.

"Thanks for not adding 'for a girl' to the end of that sentence."

"Nah, I wasn't even thinking that," he says. "Most people don't offer to help me, that's all."

Back at the van, he takes one step up and is in the back. I have to press my hands to the van floor and push myself up. I might be strong, but I'm still short. I stare at Josh as he picks up one of the two nightstands, lifting it high over his head. There's a tattoo of a robin on the inside of his arm and I wonder if it symbolizes anything, but that would be weird to ask.

He steps out of the van just as easily as he stepped into it, only this time he's holding a solid wood end table over his head. I pick up the other one, refusing to make it look like I'm struggling a little bit. I don't know why it feels like I need to prove I'm as strong as he thinks I am, but I do.

He turns to me, the nightstand still held over his head.

"You wanna race?" His voice is deep, and a little raspy, and *holy crap*.

He's cute.

I think I like him.

I think I have an actual crush on an actual guy besides Luca.

The nightstand feels ten times heavier as I set it back down at the end of the van and then hop off, my shoes hitting the concrete with a smack. I reach over and pick it back up, hoping the weight of the thing will seem like the reason my cheeks are flushing red.

"Umm, no." I walk past him. "Safety first."

"Aww, you're no fun." He keeps pace with me as we walk back to the storage area. He smells good, like fresh cucumber melon, and earthy, like taking a walk through the forest. I wonder if it's his cologne, or deodorant, or maybe a mixture of both.

"I just don't have time to get injured," I say with a quick smile. "Plus… I know you'll win."

He laughs, a deep, happy sound that's contagious. I can't help the wide, goofy grin on my face. "I wouldn't win," he says, that easy grin still lingering on his lips. "I have this fatal flaw where I always let pretty girls win."

Then it happens.

My chest. My *heart*. It does this tiny little… hiccup thing. This quick, split-second burst of adrenaline that's just like when I'm driving the box van and someone in front of me brakes too quickly and I have to slam on the brakes too, the furniture in the back flying forward, and I'm clinching my teeth, hoping and praying I don't get in a wreck. Only that's a *bad* heart flutter feeling.

This is a very *good* heart flutter feeling. Luca has called me pretty a thousand times. But it's never made my heart flutter.

Is this what it feels like to crush on someone?

Josh helps me choose patio furniture and we load it all up in the back of the van. I'm not even sure if I'm getting the right kind of stuff for the house we need to stage because I'm walking around in this weird fog. Josh and I are flirting and laughing and having a really good time. It's hard to focus on choosing modern and colorful patio furniture when there's a cute guy in your way, smelling amazing and flirting with you.

"Looks like you're ready to go," Josh says after keying the furniture tags into our business rental account. "I kind of hope Marco is out for a while. This is way more fun than assembling furniture in the sweltering heat."

"Is that your normal job?" I ask.

"One of them." He stretches out his left arm, showing me a Mexico flag tattoo that looks like a watercolor painting. "I'm also a tattoo apprentice. But that doesn't earn any money yet."

"You did that?" I say, reaching out and touching the colors that look expertly splashed across his forearm.

He nods. "Maybe another six months or so and I'll start tattooing other people."

"You're really talented."

"Thank you, Miss R&B Construction."

I laugh. "My name is Honey."

"Cute name," he says. His hands shove in his pockets. "It suits you."

Again with the unexpected compliment. We stand here just outside of the van, the summer sun shining, and time slows a little bit. I'm not entirely ready to go home yet. I think Josh feels the same. I can't believe I'm about to do this, but after yesterday's epic failure at the state park and then the mall where Maggie and I didn't talk to a single guy, my ego needs a boost.

Josh has already given me two compliments and my gut tells me he might not say no.

"You wanna go out sometime?"

Two little dimples form in his cheeks when he smiles. "How about now?"

"Aren't you working?"

He glances at the large digital clock that hangs inside the warehouse. "My shift was over half an hour ago."

"Oh no. I'm sorry I took so long."

He waves my worries away with his hand. "Not a problem. So… ice cream?"

Maybe this whole date-finding mission won't be so bad after all. The patio furniture isn't needed until tomorrow morning, so I figure I can take a little longer getting back to work. I text Jill and tell her I'm going to run some errands while I'm out because she's more forgiving of that kind of thing than my mom. Mom thinks life should be work, work, work. Jill knows there's way more to life than that. As soon as Jill replies with a thumbs up emoji, I look up at Josh and grin. "Ice cream sounds great."

We walk across the street to a place called Screaming Cream, which like the punk rock version of an ice cream shop. The walls are covered in decoupaged comic book pages, and the tables all have a collection of CDs and old school cassette tapes embedded in the tabletops with resin. I didn't even know this place existed, and it seems fitting that my first date with a new guy is at a place I've never been to before. There are no old memories of Luca inside these walls. It's all fresh and new and fills me with equal amounts of anxiety and delight.

"I'm a Jammin' Java Mocha guy myself," Josh says, tapping the glass that separates us from Screaming Cream's fifteen funkily-named ice cream flavors. "What's your poison?"

"Jammin' Java Mocha sounds pretty good."

The person behind the counter scoops our ice cream into a chocolate cookie waffle bowl, and then tops it off with whipped cream and chocolate shavings. Josh asks for extra cherries on top of his. The moment Josh takes out his wallet to pay for both of us, the weight of being on a date sinks in. This isn't just some vague idea anymore. It's real.

I think of Luca and wonder what he's doing right now. He's probably still at the jobsite, helping the dads renovate a house. A pang of guilt ripples through me and I almost drop my ice cream. Luca is working right now and I'm on a date.

Date number one.

Josh and I sit at a table with Hot Wheels race cars under the clear resin tabletop. There are at least a dozen people here, and with the music playing in the background, it's nice and loud, which means no one will overhear if I make a total idiot of myself. I don't remember if Luca and I ever had a first date. We've just always been together, always doing the same thing. By the time we were old enough to drive ourselves to have a private date, we'd already been to third base a million times so it's not like I was nervous to go on a silly date with Luca.

"Thank you for the ice cream," I say. I will not think of Luca right now.

"You're totally welcome," Josh says, that dimpled grin making me smile. "Thank you for showing up and making my day worthy of ice cream."

"You mean cherries?" I tease. "Because yours is like ninety percent cherries."

"They're the best part!" he says. He scoops a spoonful of

cherries and eats them. "All candied and not tasting at all like real fruit. Who could resist?"

I haven't stopped grinning since we got here, and I'm not sure if it's because I'm having fun or just extremely nervous. I have no idea what to say or do and I'm so scared that the conversation will wane and dreadful awkward silence will take over.

"So tell me about yourself," Josh says. He plucks another cherry off the top of his ice cream and eats it. "How long have you worked at R&B?"

"My whole life?" I say with a snort. "My parents own the place. I practically grew up there."

"Oh, right on," he says with a nod. "My parents own a restaurant. I'd rather work anywhere but there. You come home smelling like food."

"Do you come home smelling like furniture now?"

"Probably," he says, glancing up at me. "I'd rather smell like tattoo shop, though."

"Do tattoo shops have smells?"

"Not really," he says, thinking it over. "Maybe a little sterile since we sanitize everything. You have any tattoos?"

I shake my head. "I haven't been legally old enough to get one until recently."

He lifts an eyebrow. "You're eighteen?"

"How old are you?" I ask, feeling suddenly weird about this whole thing. What if he's grossly old and just doesn't look like it?

"Twenty-one."

My shoulders sink in relief. "Okay... cool."

He grins. "Would you have ran out of here if I was older?"

"Probably..." I say, biting my bottom lip.

He shrugs. "At least you're honest."

To my great relief, the conversation never sinks into dreaded awkward silence. Josh is fun and lively and he's passionate about his future career as a tattoo artist. He shows me pictures of his work on his phone. He's crazy talented. I'm a little jealous that he gets to pursue the career he wants and no one is standing in his way.

Shortly after our ice cream is gone, Josh gets a text from the owner of the tattoo shop, asking if he can come in. Josh gives me an apologetic look. "I hate to cut this date short, but if an apprentice doesn't show up, that looks really bad."

I shake my head. "No, no, you should go."

He stands up and walks with me back across the road to the furniture store. "I had a lot of fun today."

"Me too," I say, and it's not even just a polite thing to say. I really mean it. "Maybe I'll come by and get a tattoo one day."

"For sure." He reaches into his pocket. "What's your number?"

I must look weird because his smile fades. "Or email? Social? I'm not picky."

"You can text me anytime," I say, holding out my hand. He gives me his phone and I type my number on the screen.

He pockets his phone then opens the van door for me. I climb inside and close the door. He waves before turning away. Our date is officially over. My *first date* is officially over. I lean my head back against the seat and release a sigh that's been building up ever since I asked him to go out with me.

I survived a date with a cute guy. And he asked for my number! Maybe this dating thing isn't so scary after all.

Only four more to go.

CHAPTER NINE

Maggie is already waiting outside my fourth period class when the lunch bell rings. "Josh still hasn't texted me," I say as the hallways flood with people. "It's been three days!"

It turns out dating is not as fun as I thought it would be. After giving Josh my number that day at the furniture store, I sat around for three days waiting for his text. Every time my phone gets any notification at all, my heart races and I get all nervous, hoping it's him. But it's never him. It's like our date didn't even happen.

Maggie frowns. "Sorry, love."

"How'd you get here so fast?" Usually we meet in front of the library before lunch. In the week since Luca and I broke up, Maggie and I have been sitting on the other side of the cafeteria. It's the first time in all four years of high school that I haven't sat at the same table with Luca and his friends.

"We had a sub today so I snuck out," Maggie says quickly. "Let's eat outside. Can we go out this way?" She eyes a side door at the end of the hallway.

"Only the doors by the cafeteria are unlocked," I say. She

should know that by now. The only outdoors area we're allowed to go during the school day is the courtyard by the cafeteria. Get caught anywhere else and you'll get written up.

Maggie groans. "That's so far away."

It's been a week since the breakup, and while the first few days had me feeling like a circus sideshow, the constant stares and hushed whispers have mostly gone away. Or at least people started gossiping behind my back and not in front of my face. It feels different now, though. As we make our way through the crowded hallway toward the courtyard, it once again feels like it did the first day after the breakup. People are watching me.

Maggie picks up her pace. "Let's hurry."

"Why are you racing outside?" I ask, jogging to catch up to her. "What happened?"

"It doesn't matter what happened. All that matters now is that we need to find a large hole for me to jump into and never be seen again."

Maybe all those stares in the hallway are for her, not me. Maggie pushes open the double doors that lead to the courtyard and doesn't stop her powerwalk pace until we're at a picnic table that's as far as you can get from the school. She drops her backpack on the table then turns to face me. "I am such an idiot."

"What happened?" I ask again.

With her lips pressed into a thin line, she slowly inhales through her nose. "I just made a complete fool of myself in front of Shawn Beck. I finally got the courage to talk to the most gorgeous guy in school and I ruined it. I am the biggest loser on the planet."

"Slow down and talk to me," I say. I don't like that Maggie

is upset, but for once it's kind of nice that the crisis isn't about me. "It can't be that bad. What happened?"

"Oh, it's bad." She reaches up and plucks off a row of eyelashes from her eyelid. I flinch at the suddenness of it, having forgotten that she often wears fake lashes. Maggie's half-naked eye floods with tears. "I knew I shouldn't have tried these magnetic falsies on a school day!"

"They're *magnetic*?" I ask, temporarily distracted from the crisis at hand.

She nods and lifts the row of falsies back to her eyelid. It snaps into place over her eyeliner. "The company sent me a free set to review on my YouTube channel. I tried them out today and it was a huge mistake. They come off so easily."

"So what happened with Shawn?"

Maggie stress-eats a protein bar from her backpack while she tells me the whole embarrassing tale. "As you know, we have chemistry together in fourth period," she says over a mouth of food. "We had to partner up to use the microscopes. And I just told myself, you know what? Be brave. Be bold. So I asked him to be my partner. And then… I looked into the stupid microscope eyepiece and when I looked up again, Shawn says, 'what's wrong with your eye?'"

With a look of disgust, she takes the final bite of her protein bar. "My magnetic eyelashes were stuck to the eyepiece and I was sitting there in front of Shawn freaking Beck looking like this!"

She yanks off the row of eyelashes again.

"You're still beautiful," I say.

She glares at me.

"Maybe a little… uneven," I admit. The dark green eyeshadow on her left eye seems to glow at me like a streetlight now that it's not shadowed by long eyelashes. "What did Shawn say?"

"Nothing. I took my stupid falsie off the microscope, tried to laugh like it was no big deal, and then left ten minutes before the bell rang."

My eyes widen. I'd be freaking out too if the same thing happened to me. "It'll be okay," I say, hoping I sound sincere. "Shawn is a nice guy. He won't judge you for that."

She dabs the tears in her eyes with her fingers. "You know what? I don't even care. I'm going to New York in a few months, so forget him."

I know she doesn't mean that. Maggie's crush on Shawn is as strong as her passion for makeup. I want to send him a text and let him know what I should have said weeks ago—that my best friend is amazing and perfect for him—but I was too busy caught up in my boyfriend issues and worries about college to do something nice for her. This is the first time Maggie and I have actually talked in a few days because I've spent all my time watching my phone for Josh to text me.

"I'm a bad friend," I say with a sigh. "You were waiting outside my door and the first thing I did was talk about Josh instead of ask you if you're okay. I'm sorry."

Maggie smiles. It's a little pained, but she doesn't hate me. "It's no big deal. So what if we are incapable of passing the Bechtel test?"

"No, it is a big deal. I'm sick of guys. You know what?" I take my phone from my back pocket. "I'm turning this thing off. I don't care if Josh never texts me."

I unlock the screen but stop before pressing the power button. My phone has been flooded with notifications on social media and even a few texts from friends.

"What is it?" Maggie says, leaning over to look. "Whoa.

Please tell me all those aren't from Shawn telling you I'm a weirdo with disappearing eyelashes and he never wants to see me again and will definitely never date me."

"I thought you didn't care about him anymore," I say, squinting as I scroll through the notifications in the bright sunlight. "But no, it's not from him."

Leigh has texted me: *I'm here for you girl. #TeamHoney*

Aiden simply texted: *#TeamHoney #TeamHoney #TeamHoney*

My stomach drops. Why is my name a hashtag?

Maggie slides over on the bench, sitting so close to me I can smell the peanut butter on her breath. We don't say a word as I go through my phone, finally realizing what exactly caused my friends to text me messages of solidarity.

Luca went on a date last night with Lizzy McConnell, who apparently chose the last hour as the perfect time to share a dozen photos of the event on her feed. It's not surprising that he went on a date with Lizzy. She's on the girls' track team, so they're athletic friends so it makes sense that Luca would ask her out.

What's surprising is, well… how great they look together.

Luca took her to get dinner at Magic Mark's Pizzeria and then they went roller skating. Today in fourth period, Lizzy posted twenty-seven pictures chronicling the entire event, smiling her big perfect-teeth, perfect-lip-gloss smile in every single one. She looks happier than I've ever seen her. Luca also looks happy. Lizzy's hands are all over my boyfriend.

Ex-boyfriend.

I turn off my phone and shove it deep down to the bottom of my backpack, not caring if it gets crushed under the weight of my chem textbook or laptop.

"Honey?" Maggie says tentatively.

"It's fine," I say. The weird part is that I mean it. It really is fine. My stomach is in knots, but I wouldn't call myself heart-broken. It's just all so *weird*. "I went on a date, too," I say. "And I'll go on four more dates, and so will Luca. We knew this would happen."

"You really are fine?" she inquires, peering at me through squinted eyelashes.

I nod.

"Okay, because Luca is walking over here," she says under her breath, her eyes fixing behind me.

"Ugh, nooo." My cheeks get all warm.

"Keep walking," Maggie snaps at him.

I turn around and Luca halts, his eyes darting from Maggie's glare to me.

"I just wanted to say that I told her not to post those photos," Luca says. The sunlight brings out the burgundy in his dark hair, making him more boyish than man. He runs a hand over his head. "And I'm sorry everyone is making such a big deal out of nothing."

"Are you having trouble hearing?" Maggie says. She snaps her fingers. "Keep. Walking."

Luca looks at me. He's maybe twenty feet away. I haven't seen him in a few days since I've been riding to school with Maggie and avoiding him at lunch. My chest tightens at his expression. He really is upset, probably because he's getting just as many texts and messages as I am about Lizzy's sudden social media blast.

I could veto Maggie's words and tell Luca to come hang out. I could smile and pat the bench next to me and make everything totally okay again. But I don't. Every time I think about calling Luca in the middle of the night or running over to his house and throwing myself into his arms, I just stop and remember the fight we had over my dream college. If Luca and I are really going to give this break up experiment a shot, we have to stay broken up. So Maggie is right.

He can keep walking.

I've been thinking a lot about celebrities lately. Mostly how they have to put up with a barrage of rumors and tabloids and paparazzi following their every move and speculating on their every relationship. Celebrities are lucky enough to take comfort in their millions of dollars and adoring fans. I am not a celebrity. I am simply Honey Blackwell. I have fifty bucks to my name and an entire high school staring at me.

Somehow I make it to my last class of the day without running into Lizzy. She and I have never been friends—or enemies—but now the entire ecosystem of Stonebrook High has been tossed upside down and you can just see the venomous anticipation in everyone's eyes. They want us to hate each other.

I'd rather pretend my love life wasn't on display, thank you very much.

Mr. Howell's computer programming class is the most boring class anyone could have at the end of the day. I'm dreading how these last forty-five minutes of school are going to drag on for eternity, but then Mr. Howell turns off the lights and turns on the projector screen. We're watching a documentary on artificial intelligence and have to write down ten things we find interesting about it. Not bad as far as school work goes, but I doubt it will make the time go any faster.

A few minutes into the film, Chase rolls his computer chair across the aisle until he's right next to me. Chase is on the Varsity track team with Luca. He has long blond hair he keeps pulled back in a tangly ponytail and more than once I've wanted to take a hairbrush to it.

"You need a pen or something?" I whisper.

"Nah," he says, flashing me a grin. In the dim classroom, I can only see his super white teeth and the shine of his eyes. "I wanted to ask you on a date. Movies? Beach? Roller skating?" he says with an obvious tone in his voice.

I roll my eyes and focus back on my paper where I've only written one interesting fact so far.

"Yo, give me a chance," Chase says, tapping the wheels of his chair to the wheels of mine. "I'm cool. I'll treat you right."

I look right at him, hoping he catches the seriousness in my gaze. I'm not playing hard to get here. "You're one of Luca's friends."

"So what? Luca is out there dating, and so should you."

We didn't exactly say we can't date each other's friends, but I'm pretty sure it's implied. Still, I'm tempted to agree to this date just because I'm worried I won't find four more people to date before graduation. I glance at his ratty ponytail and change my mind.

"Sorry, I can't. It would be way too awkward."

Mr. Howell clears his throat and casts a pointed glance in our direction. Chase rolls his chair back a few inches then whispers, "If you change your mind..." He points to himself with a grin.

I rest my forehead on my palm, my eyes wide with disbelief over what just happened. When I look up again, I notice someone watching me from a few desks over. It's Mason, leaned back in his chair, his feet propped up on the desk. He doesn't wave or nod or acknowledge me. He's just watching me, his face covered in shadows from the projector light that's dancing around the dark room. I know he saw everything, but I doubt he heard any of it. I spend a few seconds wondering how he could use this info to poke fun at me during the next STEM Club meeting.

Then I look away, deciding I don't really care.

CHAPTER TEN

The sky is a perfect Friday evening deep blue, the horizon still illuminated by the last rays of the setting sun. The air is filled with the smell of barbequed ribs and spicy seasoned corn on the cob. The dads work the grill and the moms sit on the porch swing sharing a bottle of wine. Aunt Bree is on her way over and Maggie is already here. Flames dance in the stone firepit while Maggie and I sit around it in bright blue Adirondack chairs. It's a typical Friday night, minus one person: Luca.

Maggie sips her cherry Coke from a bendy straw she's inserted into the hole on the pop tab, which she twisted around to cover the opening of the can. "So that gigantic a-hole never called?"

I shake my head, resisting the urge to check my phone once more for something from Josh. "Never called. Never texted. Never found me on social media."

"Oh well. Four more dates to find your soulmate," she says, relaxing back in the chair. "You have your sights set on anyone?"

"Nope." I haven't told her about Chase's proposition yesterday because he doesn't count. He's too close to Luca's friend circle and not exactly my type.

Country music plays from the outdoor speaker because it's Tony's turn to play DJ tonight. All the songs on his phone's playlists are country, mostly the old school stuff I enjoy like Garth Brooks or George Strait. My favorite grill nights are when the moms or Luca get to control the music because we all like the same things. The dads are the only two die-hard country music fans in the family.

"Bree's here!" Mom calls out in her slightly tipsy singsong voice. My aunt waves as she crosses from our backyard into Luca's where we're hanging out tonight.

"I brought cookies," she says, stopping in front of Maggie and me to hold out the plastic tub of mint chocolate chip. These soft baked cookies with chocolate chips and bits of Andes mints are her second specialty, right after brookies. "Take a bunch before your dad eats them all."

"Hey! No cookies until after dinner," Dad calls out. "Better bring me them to me for safe keeping."

"My Honey is a college girl now," Aunt Bree says, setting the cookie tub in my lap. "She can eat dessert for dinner in Colorado and no one will know."

I straighten. The Colorado thing isn't exactly welcome conversation around our house. My parents still think I'm going to A&M with Luca in the fall.

Dad snorts and peaks underneath the foil on the grill. "Honey, are you still considering that school?"

I glance at Maggie, who looks just as uncomfortable as I do. She may be my best friend, but she can't save me from this conversation. Not unless she fakes a heart attack or something... when she does nothing of the sort, I look at my dad.

"I don't know. Kind of."

He scoffs.

"Oh hush, Blaine," Mom says. "I think Colorado is a great idea."

"She's going to A&M," Dad says. "We all went there, Luca is going there, and Honey is going there. It's tradition and it's a hell of a lot closer and cheaper than some frou-frou school in Colorado."

"I can help her pay for it," Aunt Bree says. She's never one to back down to my dad, no matter how intimidating everyone else thinks he is. "It's her dream school and she should go."

"The money is only one part of the issue," Dad says, pointing his grilling tongs in my direction. "I love you, kid, but this college came out of nowhere. It's not like you can't get a perfectly good education here in Texas. Amber? Back me up here?"

Mom focuses on removing the bottle opener from the cork in her hand. "Honey should do whatever she wants to do."

"Unbelievable," Dad mutters.

"Aww, come on." Tony cracks open the top of a new beer can and takes a long sip. His mannerisms are so similar to Luca's, which has never bothered me until now. "It's Honey's decision and we shouldn't make it for her."

"Where the hell is Luca?" Dad says. "He'll be on my side."

"Can we please just drop this?" I say before anyone can tell my dad that Luca is out on a date with someone who isn't me. Just like the college thing, Dad also thinks the breakup thing isn't anything to worry about. As far as he's concerned, everything in our lives is still perfectly in the status quo. "Maggie doesn't need to be subjected to our drama."

"For real," Mom says with a lighthearted laugh.

"Sorry," Dad says, flashing Maggie an apologetic smile. "I didn't mean to annoy everyone. Let's eat."

These backyard grill nights are a summer staple in the Rollins-Blackwell households. Now that the random Texas cold fronts seem to have faded away, replaced by hot summer days, we can expect to have dinner out here every single Friday and some Saturdays too. It didn't occur to me until this very moment, sitting around the firepit with Maggie and my family, that if I go away to college, I will miss out on traditions like this. If Luca and I break up for good, what happens to backyard grill nights? Will Luca bring a new girlfriend out here one day and then *I'll* be the missing piece of the tradition?

I keep my thoughts to myself since the conversation has successfully moved onto boring things like sports and mosquito repellant. Maggie and I eat around the fire. I try to pay attention to her story about some rare Egyptian makeup book she's been trying to find online, but my thoughts are all over the place. I can't remember a time I ate dinner in the backyard without Luca nearby.

"I love springtime in the states," Maggie says after we've downed entirely too many mint chocolate chip cookies. She kicks back in her chair, resting her sandals on another chair next to her. "It's so much prettier outside than in London."

"If the allergies don't kill you," Dad says. He's sitting on the other side of the bonfire, beer in one hand and the other hand holding Mom's. "One of these days I'm going to pack up the family business and move to Arizona. There's no pollen nightmare in that desert state."

"Keep talking shit, old man," Luca's dad says. "No one believes that Arizona talk, no matter how much you say it. We are Texans, through and through."

"Aren't you both the same age?" Maggie asks.

Tony snorts. "Age is just a number. I'm the more handsome, younger-looking man here so he'll always be the old man. Not me."

"You're both old," Jill says. There aren't enough Adirondack chairs to go around, so she's sitting in Tony's lap.

Mom raises her wine glass appreciatively. "I second that observation."

"And what does that make you two since we were all born in the same year?" Dad says playfully.

Jill doesn't miss a beat. "Beautiful, ageless, queens."

She holds out her hand and Mom high-fives her.

"Your life is so cool," Maggie says.

I don't even know how to respond. It's true that my parents are cool and my life is pretty good. That's how it's always been around here. Happy go-lucky parents and constant jokes and fun, all wrapped around decades of family tradition. Everyone has a good time because no one deviates from what's expected of us.

And yet... if at the end of these two months, Luca and I decide we aren't soulmates, we'll be doing just that.

Deviating.

CHAPTER ELEVEN

"Whoa." I pause the television right when a shirtless Mac Carlson appears on the screen. "Aiden was right. You are basically his twin."

"My abs are better," Luca says, scrutinizing the TV. "And my legs. And my hair. Wow, maybe I should be the famous actor here."

I snort a laugh and toss a Cheeto at him. "Try not to be so incredibly humble."

Luca and I are binge-watching the newest season of our show. It's funny how quickly we slip back into our comforting routines after two weeks of being apart. Granted, I'm sitting on the recliner and not cuddled up next to him on the couch, but it's basically a normal weekend around here. Maybe that's the problem, though. If we can break up and still be the same, maybe we were never meant to be together in the first place.

"So how many dates have you been on?" Luca asks during the twenty seconds before the next episode plays.

"One." It's the same number of dates I said when he asked me a week ago.

His eyes flash with surprise for just a second before he reaches for his soda can on the coffee table. "You better get on it. Only five weeks left until you realize we're soulmates."

"Confident and humble! What about you?" I prod. "How many dates have you been on if you're so sure we're soulmates?"

"Two, but it's two more than I need to know you're the girl for me."

My stomach tightens. Not just because he's confirmed what I already suspected—that he missed the last BBQ night because he'd been on a date—but also because he's so set on us being soulmates no matter what.

"You're going to ruin the experiment if you refuse to give it a real shot."

"I am giving it a shot," Luca says, peering at me over his soda. "I've been on twice as many dates as you so maybe I'm actually taking this breakup more seriously."

I roll my eyes. "Dating isn't easy. I can't just snap my fingers and get a date."

Luca flops backward on the leather couch, his arms stretching out across both empty seats next to him. "Sure you can. You know how many guys on the team wish they had the guts to ask you out?"

"Chase already did," I say, curling my lip.

"What's wrong with Chase?"

"He's your friend?" My voice sounds exactly the way I feel —like he's dumb for even asking.

Luca shrugs. "We're not best friends or anything. I have a date with Leigh this week so it's basically the same thing.

"You're going out with Leigh?"

"She was giving so many hints it was impossible to miss," he says as if that answers my question. I shouldn't care so much, but Leigh isn't like Lizzy. She's not some random girl who goes to my school. Leigh is my friend. Just a couple weeks ago she was oogling my boyfriend right in front of me at the track meet.

"If you don't want me to go out with her I can cancel," Luca says with all the enthusiasm of someone who definitely does not want to cancel.

I shake my head. "I don't care. It's just weird, that's all."

"You should go out with Chase and then it'll be even."

"Maybe," I say. I should have done more research on this science experiment. If the goal is to find your soulmate, then surely I should only go out with guys I actually like. Chase is not a guy I like. But maybe I don't know what kind of guys I like because I've never really thought about it. I've never had a crush on anyone, besides maybe a K-pop star or actor like Mac Carlson, because I've always had Luca.

The pressure to catch up to Luca's three dates weighs heavily on me. While our show plays, I think about Chase. He would be cute if he brushed his hair and he seems nice enough. I don't really know much else about him. For all I know, he could be my soulmate in disguise. While pretending to watch the TV, I pull up Chase's social media account and send him a message, typing quickly before I chicken out.

Me: Still up for that date?
Chase: Any time, any place. :D

We decide on dinner and rock climbing. Chase promises it'll be fun even though I've never climbed anything higher than the kitchen counter when I need to reach something in a top cabinet. I am nervous, but happy to at least have date number two ready to go. Still, it feels like dating should be more fun than just checking off boxes.

If I'm going to give this experiment a chance to prove if Luca is my real soulmate or not, I should try to go on a date with someone I have a genuine, real crush on. Someone who is more of my personality than Luca's. Someone who likes science and nature walks instead of running track and playing video games. A face appears in my mind. Heart-shaped with longish black hair and a smirky grin. It's some kind of joke my subconscious is playing on me, no doubt. I shake the image away. *Not today, brain.*

I'm trying to find a soulmate.

Not my biggest enemy.

CHAPTER TWELVE

A few days ago I had no idea ancient Egyptians even had makeup routines. Now I know all about it, thanks to Maggie's recent obsession. She's deep into her unspoken YouTube fight with Makeup Maria, and she's absolutely positive that the only way she'll win this war is by getting her hands on the coveted and extremely rare Ancient Egyptian makeup book so she can revitalize the earliest trends and transform the makeup world as we know it. Unfortunately the only copy we've found is on eBay for twelve hundred dollars.

"I told Mum it was basically part of my college education to have this book but she refuses to give me the money for it," Maggie says, her bottom lip jutting out in a pout. "She thinks if the book was good enough the publisher would have printed way more copies. But it's not the author's fault that people don't respect ancient Egyptian techniques as much as they should!"

"I'm really sorry, Mags. If I had the money, that book would be yours."

Maggie rests her cheek on my shoulder while we walk down the crowded school hallways. "You're the best."

"Hey, Honey." I hear the voice before I see who said it. Chase weaves around people until he's walking in step with us. He grins like a little kid and swipes the blonde hair flyaways back over his forehead. "You want a ride home after school?"

"I already have a ride," I say, sheepishly nodding toward Maggie. "But thanks."

"No worries. I'll pick you up at six?"

I nod. Dating is awkward.

Chase grins again. He has a dimple in his left cheek but not the other one. "Cool. See you then."

I can feel Maggie staring at me as Chase disappears into the crowd. "That's Chase?"

"Yep."

"…Cute."

"You hesitated a lot for a one word reply."

She laughs. "I'm still getting used to the idea of you dating. It's weird. But a good weird. You want me to do your makeup after school?"

"No," I say, stopping at the corner by the English hallway. This is where we part ways before sixth period. "I want to be casual for this date."

She nods as if she's some all-knowing oracle. "Make sure you call me right after the date so you can tell me all about it."

I turn back around to head to my sixth period, but the overpowering stare of two freshman girls stops me in my tracks. It's clear they've just seen this exchange with Chase and Maggie and now they're judging me for it. Or maybe it's not clear. Maybe I'm just inventing things in my head because the look one of the girls gives me seems like it's saying, *You went from Luca to him? That's such a downgrade.*

"So what?" I snap at their unvoiced opinion. The girls flinch.

I head to class.

Maggie drops me off at home after school and I practically have to beg her to leave or else she might hold me down and do my makeup for me. As much as I appreciate her makeover skills, I don't want them tonight. This date with Chase is just Date Number Two. It's nothing special. Nothing worth getting all dressed up for.

I was hoping my parents would still be at work this evening. It's not unusual that one or both of them are still up at the R&B offices until well after seven. But since Fate hates me, and all my good luck got used up when FLU accepted me, both Mom and Dad get home right at 5:15, as if they actually work normal hours.

"Mom, Dad," I say, cornering them in the living room five minutes before six. "I'm going on a date tonight. He'll be here soon, so don't get weird about it."

"What kind of date?" Dad asks.

"Dinner and rock climbing at that indoor place off the interstate."

"Humph." Dad shakes his head. "Don't go breakin' some kid's heart now. He should know he doesn't stand a chance."

"Don't let your heart get broken either," Mom says.

"It's just a stupid date," I say. "It's dinner and rock climbing. No hearts are getting broken. You act like I'm going off to star on an episode of the Bachelor or something."

The doorbell rings. Oh great. He's going to be polite and walk up to my door. Why couldn't he have just waited in the car?

I rush to the door but Dad beats me to it. "Hello there," Dad says, holding out his large, calloused hand. "I'm Blaine Blackwell."

"Chase Carmichael. Nice to meet you, sir."

I shove past my dad and see Chase standing on our porch. He's wearing khaki cargo shorts and a dark blue button up shirt. His hair has been brushed and pulled into a neat ponytail at the base of his neck. I've never seen his hair this tame before.

"Ready to go?" I ask quickly so this conversation doesn't last any longer than absolutely necessary.

"Hold on," Mom calls out. "I want to meet this gentleman."

I reluctantly step out onto the porch, making way for my mom. She smiles at him. "How do you know Honey?"

Chase smiles right back. If he's nervous, he doesn't look like it. "We go to school together."

"Wonderful," Mom says. "You two have a fun time."

"Be home by midnight," Dad says.

"It's a school night!" Mom tells him.

"Eleven, then," Dad amends.

After what feels like hours, the front door closes and we're making our way to Chase's Tacoma. "I'm so sorry about my parents."

He snorts. "That was nothing. Your parents are nice. You wouldn't believe how many dads tell me I should cut my hair. Some even offer to do it for me."

"Wow."

"This one girl's dad lectured me for twenty minutes before

letting me take his daughter out for ice cream. He told me if I wanted to see her again, I'd come back with a respectable haircut."

I laugh. "Something tells me that relationship didn't last."

"I barely made it through the ice cream."

Rick's Rock Climbing is located across town in a huge metal warehouse. I've never been inside but I've seen their advertisements on Instagram. There are five different climbing walls ranging from a little kid wall to a complex terrifying thing that I'm pretty sure you'd need to have a death wish to climb.

I stare in awe and fear as we make our way to the cash register at the front of the facility. One person climbs all the way to the top of the scary wall without a harness. Their muscles flex, showing off their incredible strength.

"That's my goal," Chase says, gesturing toward the climber. "I'm going to master the mountain before summer is over."

"Without a rope?"

"Without a rope," he says, cracking his knuckles. "I can already make it up there easy with a rope."

"Easy?" someone says behind the counter. "You mean *barely*."

"Not cool, man," Chase says to the guy behind the counter. His nametag says Ryan and he's a tall Black guy with a short afro.

Ryan smiles at me. "I'm just playing. Chase is a cool dude. He's a great rock climber, too. Probably the best climber to ever step foot in here. I'm surprised he hasn't won any gold medals."

"Now you're taking it too far," Chase says.

Ryan chuckles and taps the touch screen on the register. "Two passes?"

"Yep." Chase takes out his wallet.

"I'll pay for mine," I say softly so only he can hear.

"Psh, no way." Chase hands over his card and Ryan stamps our hands. Chase has a backpack full of climbing gear for himself, but I couldn't be more unaware of how this whole thing works so Ryan takes me to the room next to the registers. We find a harness in my size and I learn how to put the thing on. Then I get shoes and a little fanny pack bag of chalk powder.

Chase walks me over to the beginner wall which is about twenty feet tall and covered in colorful knobs and pieces to step on. A little girl and her dad are also using this wall. The dad stands on the floor holding onto the rope while the girl climbs from one colorful step to the next.

"This is the baby wall," I whisper.

"It's a *beginner* wall," Chase says. "You've never done this before, right?"

I shake my head.

"So I'll teach you the ropes then we'll go to the next wall. Hey," he says with a snort as he tugs on a black rope that's suspended from the ceiling with a pulley system. "I'm teaching you the *literal* ropes."

I roll my eyes. "Dork."

He gives me a quick rundown of how rock climbing works. Seems simple enough, so long as you're strong. The rope will catch me if I let go of the wall (or, let's face it, fall).

"You ready?" Chase says, hooking the rope into the clip at my waist.

"Yes." I hold up my finger and narrow my eyes. "You are not allowed to tell anyone if I embarrass myself."

He smirks then makes a solemn nod. "I won't say a word."

"Good." I turn around and face the wall. Colorado has real rock faces for climbing. Maybe this can be good practice. It takes me longer than the little girl beside me, but I do make it all the way to the top of the beginner wall. I smack the button at the top and it lights up. Success.

We move on to the next wall, which juts out in a few places, making it not just a simple straight climb, but more of a perilous journey. Chase is clearly trying to impress me when he climbs up the wall in record time, his grin so big he has dimples in both cheeks. It kind of works. I am impressed, but I'm not sure that means he's my soulmate. This is still just a simple date, not a love connection.

After a few trial and errors and one massive Charlie horse cramp in my calf, I manage to make it to the top of the second wall. I smack the button and then let go of the wall. Chase guides the rope to allow me to slowly fall back to earth.

"You're amazing," he says, helping unhook the rope from my harness. "You're a natural rock climber."

"I wonder how hard real rocks are compared to this." I'm a little out of breath and definitely a bit sweaty. I stretch my arms over my head to wring out my muscles.

"I wouldn't know. There aren't any good cliff faces around here," Chase says with a snort."

"There are in Colorado."

"You go there a lot?"

I shake my head. "Never been, but I got accepted to my dream school in Colorado. Fault Line University."

"Nice," he says, holding out his fist. I bump my knuckles to his. "I love hearing stories of people getting out of this dumb town."

"Totally," I say. This is the first time I've mentioned FLU as if it's a college I'm actually going to and not just having a total identity crisis over because I'm not sure if should go or not. It feels good to say it like it's the truth. Maybe it will be.

"You ready for dinner?" Chase nods toward the burger restaurant that's next door. It's actually connected to the rock climbing facility with a long bar and a set of glass doors that lead into the restaurant.

"I'm starving."

The Burger Shack isn't just your regular burger joint. They have off-the-wall names for every burger on the menu and the walls are covered in photos, memorabilia, and dollar bills. We go up to the counter to order and once again Chase takes out his wallet.

I know it's some kind of outdated dating rule that guys always pay, but Luca and I never really did that. We both work at the same place and have about the same amount of money, so we randomly take turns paying, or we each pay for our own stuff when we go out.

"I'll buy our food," I say.

"No way."

"You got the rock climbing, I'll get dinner. It's only fair."

"It's on me." When I go to object, Chase puts his hands on my shoulders. "Look. I know about the experiment with Luca. I know you're probably going to get back with him at the end of all your dates and that's probably why you want to pay so you don't feel like you're leading me on or whatever. But I don't care. I still want to take you out on a date. Please let me pay and treat you like a princess for a night."

My teeth dig into my bottom lip. That was possibly the sweetest thing ever. I never in a million years of classes together would I have imagined Chase is capable of saying something that romantic. Besides those few seconds of my parents embarrassing me at our front door, I haven't exactly been nervous tonight. The awkward tingle of apprehension starts tickling my skin.

"Okay," I say, releasing my bottom lip from my teeth. "Thank you."

CHAPTER THIRTEEN

Anna is a few minutes late to STEM Club on Friday, but she makes up for it by bringing pizzas from Magic Mark's. She sets the two boxes down on the table and then stands up, shoulders back while she makes spirit fingers in front of the food. "Free pizza! Courtesy of my manager Jan. She gives me pizza coupons every time I help her clean the fryers."

"Thank you, Jan!" Vu says. He opens the top box and grabs a slice of pizza that's covered in every topping imaginable. Janise and Anna take a slice, too.

Anna laughs when she sees my face. "Don't worry, the other pizza is boring."

I lift the lid, happy to see an extra-large cheese pizza. I may have the food palette of a five-year-old, but I have no idea how anyone can enjoy mushrooms and onions on a pizza.

"I am also on team boring pizza," Mason says, reaching for a slice.

"Everything is set for this weekend," Janise says, using her pinky to open her notebook. The rest of her fingers are probably covered in pizza grease. "We have two hotel rooms right next to each other. Vu and Mason in one. Me, Honey, and Anna in the other."

She looks up at me, lowering her pizza slice. "Sorry, I uh, assumed Luca isn't coming with us anymore?"

"Oh." *How did I forget about that?* I think about texting him real quick, but then decide against it. Broken up means broken up. I shake my head. "No, he's not coming."

When we signed up for this conference months ago, the only way my parents would agree to me driving four hours away and staying in a hotel with no adults was if Luca came with me. I guess they figured we'd be less likely to get murdered if we were together. That's just straight up sexist if you ask me. I'm totally capable of not being murdered without Luca's help.

Lunch is only forty minutes long so we spend most of the club meeting eating pizza and sharing our excitement for the conference. We'll be leaving first thing tomorrow morning. Janise passes out a full itinerary for the event, even though I'm pretty sure we've all memorized the panels and exhibits well before today. I know I have. There are two geology panels I can't wait to attend. Fault Line University is one of the sponsors. Maybe I can snag an FLU T-shirt as a consolation prize if I don't end up attending in the fall.

"Have you accepted your admission yet?" Mason says over a mouthful of pizza, like he's some kind of caveman instead of one of the smartest guys in school.

How does he always seem to read my mind? I shrug. "No."

"Honey!" Anna says, eyes wide like I just said something scandalous. "You only have a couple weeks until Decision Day." She says *Decision Day* as if it's some mystical event worthy of having the words capitalized.

I take a big bite of cheese pizza but that doesn't buy me

enough time for the group to change topics. They're all watching me. I swallow. "I'm still deciding."

Mason snorts.

"You have something to say?" I snap.

"Stay here in stupid Stonebrook, or go to Colorado," he says, taking another bite of pizza. "It shouldn't even be a decision. It should be obvious."

"Everyone is on their own journey," Anna says. "Honey will choose the path that's best for her."

I wish I didn't have to choose. I wish there was just some magical, incontrovertible, way of knowing which path my life should take. Stay in Stonebrook, go to my parents' college, marry Luca, and work at R&B forever? Or go to Colorado and become an entirely different person?

Vu is never one for personal talk, so that's probably why he plays a NASA video on his phone, turning up the volume enough for everyone to hear it.

Anna scoots her chair closer to me and whispers, "You know what's really exciting? You're single now, so you'll get to check out all the hot convention goers."

I chuckle. "Yeah, I guess you're right."

"How many dates have you been on so far?"

"Two."

"Just two?" This time she forgets to whisper.

"It's a lot harder than you'd think to find guys to date," I mumble, reaching for another slice of pizza. I'm not really hungry anymore but I need something to make me feel better about my pathetically low date count.

"Well tomorrow is the first night of the convention and we will find you a hot date, right Janise?"

Janise looks up from her notebook. "Huh?"

Anna rolls her eyes. "Nothing." She turns back to me and

grabs my arm, squeezing it a little. "There are college students at this thing. Maybe we can both snag one."

I smile. "Maybe."

The moms take me out to get Chinese food for dinner because the guys and Luca will be working late on some house renovation that's over budget and taking longer than it should. Our waiter is super cute. He has short black hair and gorgeous eyes and I'm pretty sure he's giving me flirtatious smiles every time he comes by our table, but I am so not about to ask for a guy's number in front of the moms. So I cut my losses and try to daydream about the STEM conference guys Anna swears I'll meet. If I don't go on a third date soon, I might get so desperate I end up asking out a freshman.

Later, I'm packing my clothes for the long weekend in Houston when Maggie calls me on video chat. Both of her eyes are heavily covered in makeup, but in different styles. She's currently very upset that neither one looks good enough to pass as Egyptian-inspired.

"I dunno," I say, staring at my phone while it rests on top of my dresser. "The left eye looks very Cleopatra-esque."

Maggie groans, rolling her eyes back in her head. "That's exactly what it's not supposed to look like. I don't want to be some stereotyped caricature of the greatest Egyptian ruler of all time. I want to be authentic."

A text message notification appears over Maggie's face. The first thing I notice is the puke emoji at the end of Janise's text.

"Let me call you back," I tell Maggie.

Janise: Are you extremely sick right now?
Me: No..?
Janise: All of STEM Club except you and Mason
are sick. Food poisoning it seems like. Must
have been the supreme pizza. You and Mason
just had the cheese pizza.
Me: wow, that's awful.

Turns out my instincts of hating all those extra toppings have saved me a night of misery. Boring pizza for the win!

Janise: yeah so Anna and I are on the same
page… there's no way we can go to the
conference tomorrow. Vu is going to wait it
out and see what he feels like in the morning,
but most likely it'll just be you and Mason.

My lip curls.

Me: Noooooooooooo. I need you guys there!
Janise: Sorry! Take lots of pictures!

I drop my phone on the bed and stare at the black leather suitcase I borrowed from Jill. This weekend was supposed to be fun and educational and spent with Janise and Anna, my two closest friends from STEM Club. I didn't plan on seeing Mason at all.

I pick up my phone but realize I don't have Mason's number. Then I check Instagram and Snapchat and we aren't friends on there, either. I don't have any way to contact him. Sure, I could try to find his social media, or just ask Janise because she knows everything about STEM Club and its members, but I decide against it.

I've been looking forward to this conference for months and I won't let Mason ruin it. I'll just go by myself and hope we never have to cross paths. The only guys I want to talk to this weekend are cute nerdy strangers who are worthy of being date number three.

And maybe even date number four.

CHAPTER FOURTEEN

"You're *really* going alone," Mom says. It's not a question. She heaves a sigh and pinches the bridge of her nose. "Why did everyone have to get sick? I don't know why Luca can't just go with you."

"Mom, I'll be fine without him. It's only a four hour drive."

"It's not the driving I'm worried about," Mom says. "You'll be all alone in that massive city!"

"One other person from my STEM Club will be there, Mom. I'll only be in the hotel. It's not like I'll be wandering the streets of downtown Houston all alone at night."

Mom's eyes widen as if that idea hadn't occurred to her before but now she's absolutely positive that's exactly what will happen.

Beside her, Dad is standing with his arms crossed over his chest, giving me this look like I'm a little kid and I've just asked to do something stupid and he knows I'll back out any second now. "You've never left town before."

"I'm eighteen, Dad. I'll be fine."

Dad's lips press into a thin line. "If this is your idea of

teenage rebellion, I guess we got lucky. You could be on drugs, but instead you're insisting on a pointless weekend away from home." He chuckles then puts an arm around Mom's shoulders. "I guess we've raised her pretty well."

I want to tell him that it's not a pointless trip. That it'll be educational and fun and maybe even a way to help me decide if I want to accept my dream college or just play it safe and stay here. But I know better than to start an argument right now, when they're agreeing to let me go.

Dad's jaw flexes. "You be careful, Honey."

"She'll be fine," Mom says as if she's suddenly on my side. I swear, I don't get my parents. Not at all. "I wish Luca was going with her, but she'll be fine."

"I can do stuff without Luca," I mutter. "Believe it or not, I can do things *all by myself*."

Dad reaches for my suitcase, but to punctuate my point, I take it first and heft it into the trunk of Mom's car, which she's letting me borrow for the weekend.

"Love you, kid," Dad says. He's still grumpy. Still wearing that perma-scowl he's had since I told him about Fault Line University. But when he hugs me, he squeezes me extra tight and I know he still loves me. That's what makes all of this so hard. It would almost be easier if my parents just got mad and disowned me. If Luca jumped on board too and said he didn't love me anymore. Then I could leave the family and go to my dream college without feeling so awful about it.

Mom hugs me next, but her hug is quick, lacking all sentimental warm fuzzies that Mom hugs are supposed to have. "Drive safely."

My parents turn to go back inside and now I'm standing out here in the early morning sunrise staring at Luca, who just emerged from his house. He's wearing flannel pajama pants and a Dallas Cowboys shirt. His hair is ten kinds of sideways and his grin is just as crooked.

"You didn't have to wake up this early to say goodbye. You could have texted me."

"Yes I did. Before this temporary breakup, I would have been out here. So I'm out here now."

Temporary.

Is that all it is? A silly experiment where the results will be inconclusive and nothing will change and I'll forever look back on that time in my life where I almost did something cool, but it was all just temporary?

I exhale and hold out my arms. "Hug?"

Luca's body leans against mine. His long, lean arms wrap around me and hold me for a moment. This is the most contact we've had since we broke up. I close my eyes and breathe in the scent of him, and try really, really hard to feel something other than familiarity. I want a spark, a toe tingle. A warm mushy love feeling. Something bursting awake in my soul that tells me Luca is my soulmate after all.

But when we pull apart a few moments later, all it feels like is a hug. A friendly goodbye before a journey.

"Be careful. Drive safe."

"Why does everyone keep saying that? I'm a good driver."

"You just rarely ever drive," he says sheepishly. "I'm not being mean...I'm just looking out for you."

I offer him a small smile of gratitude. "Thanks—" I catch myself before saying *babe*, because that's how I used to talk to him. Old habits are hard to break, but they have to be broken if we want to give this dating experiment a real shot.

Luca is under no obligation to play the role of boyfriend now that my parents are gone, but that doesn't stop him from standing in my driveway watching me drive away. He gets smaller and smaller in the rear-view mirror, until I turn out of the neighborhood and lose sight of him.

This STEM conference is the real deal, and I am wholly unprepared for it. After finding the hotel that's nestled deep in the center of downtown Houston, with its tricky one-way streets and horrifyingly self-centered drivers, I want to take a nap instead of dive into the day's events. It makes me cringe when I remember Luca's words to me. *You just rarely ever drive.*

I rarely ever do anything I want to do, now that I think about it. Maybe I should get my own car and start doing more things on my own instead of relying on him for everything. I'm exhausted from the drive and stress of finding this place, but I'm not about to wimp out and succumb to the nap that's beckoning me. This conference is the first thing I've done for myself, and I'm going to make it count.

After dropping my things in my hotel room and doing a little dance around the room because it's the first time I've ever had a hotel to myself, I go downstairs to the conference center and sign in, get my name badge, and slip into the large ballroom just in time for the keynote speech.

The room must have five hundred people in it, most of them high school students like me. Almost everyone has a laptop or backpack with them, and I'm kicking myself for leaving my stuff in my hotel room. Maybe my dad is right, that I'm doing all of this as some kind of spontaneous teenage rebellion and I have no idea what I actually want in life. But then I remember the talk I had with the woman who visited my school from FLU. It was just a quick conversation, but I'd left her table feeling so inspired. Hearing her talk her about geophysics had opened up this part of my life I didn't know existed. Discovering Fault Line University was like finding the piece of me that was missing.

I hold onto that feeling while I listen to the keynote speech, and half an hour later, I'm feeling more inspired than ever. There is more to this life than growing old in the same town you were born in while working at a job that was designated for you when you were a kid. There's an entire world out there. I want to see as much of it as I can.

I dart up to my hotel room and grab my laptop after the keynote, then I sit in on two more panels before for lunch. I take photos and notes and send them to Janise and Anna. The conference has so many things going on at once that you can't really see it all, so I choose the panels that are related to geophysics and earth sciences. There's also a robotics competition tonight that has nothing to do with my future degree, but everyone in my STEM Club was excited about it. Most of us would have been in different panels all day, but we had all agreed to meet up tonight and watch the robots fight each other. The least I can do for the club is take pictures and watch homemade robots smash each other to bits.

Lunch is provided in one of the smaller conference rooms. It's a buffet style menu, spread out on several tables. I wander through them, filling my plate with some of everything that looks good. Since we're in Texas, the food matches all of our stereotypical Texan food. I get some mac and cheese, garlic mashed potatoes, cornbread, and smoked brisket with sugary BBQ sauce.

The tables are packed with peopled clumped together in groups of two or more. Some groups even wear matching T-shirts so they can find each other in the crowds. The students here have planned this event for months. I bet they planned college in the same way—careful, precise steps to attain their goal. Not random applications mailed in just before the deadline to a school your family doesn't want you to attend.

If I do go to FLU, will I feel just as lonely there as I do at this conference? My roommate will probably be some super smart academic type who already has friends and a plan for their life. Will leaving Stonebrook for Colorado mean being totally alone for four years?

"Would you like some company?"

No one has talked to me since I got here, and I'm not expecting anyone to talk to me now, but Mason's voice is so familiar I jump at the sound of it.

He's wearing a black button up shirt over dark jeans. He still has those thin strands of leather bracelets that he wears every day, but his black hair has been put in place with some kind of hair product. It swoops perfectly over to the side and isn't all in his face like usual. He almost looks like a different person.

"You're welcome to sit here," I say, picking up my fork. Relief floods over me at the familiar face and the idea that I won't be eating lunch alone, but I'm not about to let him know that.

"Thanks," he says, sitting down across from me. "I've been looking for you all morning. Did you know we don't have each other's phone numbers?"

I tilt my head as if the thought never occurred to me. "We don't? Weird."

His brows narrow as he reads my badge. "Wait, Honey is your real name?"

"Of course it's my real name."

"Like, legal name? I always thought it was some kind of nickname."

I shrug. "You're named after a type of jar."

Mason grins, revealing a little dimple in his left cheek. "I didn't mean it in a bad way. I think it's cool that your real name is Honey. Is there a story behind it?"

"When my mom was pregnant with me, she was obsessed with honey. Had to put it on everything. And then she started calling me Honey after I was born. A few days later, they put it on my birth certificate." I'm keenly aware of Mason's eyes on me while I talk, even though I'm focusing on my mac and cheese. I don't really like telling this story. It makes my parents sound so boring and unoriginal. My name was given to me out of a dumb joke based on Mom's pregnancy cravings.

"I can relate," he says after a beat. "My mom was obsessed with mason jars when I was born."

"Really?" I lift a skeptical brow. I think this is the most we've ever talked that wasn't about science.

He grins, bringing that one dimple back. "Nah. I'm named after my uncle. Sir Masonic Jarsmith. Inventor of the Mason jar."

I give him a look.

"What?" he says. "Some people find my jokes funny."

I roll my eyes, but I can't help myself from smiling. Mason's jokes don't have to be funny. The way he tells them makes me want to smile. He has this easy-going vibe about him, like he's the kind of person who never gets stressed out. That's just how he always is, which is infuriating when he's disagreeing with me, but funny when he's telling jokes.

"So," he says after a few moments of silent eating, "have you sent in your acceptance yet?"

"You can go sit somewhere else now."

He grins, looking down at his food. "I'm just making sure you don't forget. The due date is just around the corner."

"I am aware."

Another few moments of silence pass. Mason stabs a hush-puppy with his fork. It makes me wonder if he's ever eaten one before. They're a finger food at my house. "I'm glad I found you. It's better having a friend at a place like this."

"I'd hardly call us friends," I say, bringing my sarcasm back into the conversation to drown out my anxieties over the looming acceptance date. Mason is weirdly cute in a setting that is not Stonebrook High. It's unnerving. It's in my best interest to hide all forms of weakness around him, so I need to shove that thought straight out of my mind.

"You mean years of hostile conversation during STEM Club doesn't qualify us as friends?" Mason puts a hand to his chest. "You and your high friendship standards, Honey Black-well. Guess I'll have to try harder. What's next on your schedule?"

"I'm going to the precious metals exhibit, and then some panels on mining and explosive engineering. I'm pretty sure I want to study geophysics, but those sound cool too."

"Right on. Blowing shit up has to be a fun way to make a living. Wish I could go to that." He pulls out a paper from his pocket and unfolds it on the table. There's a list written on it in big, looping handwriting. A few of the items are already crossed out. "My mother is making me attend these lectures," he says, spinning the paper toward me.

I skim the list, but none of them are on my own itinerary of things I wanted to attend.

"I would skip out on some of them, but…" He sucks in air through his teeth. "She'll quiz me. She always does. She didn't even go to school in this country, much less college, but you better believe she's memorized every inch of the confer-ence program. *You will be the pride of our family, son.*"

"I take it you come from a strict family?"

He laughs. "Not strict, but hopeful. I'll be the first one in the family to go to college and my mom is so excited she's kind of gone overboard in trying to prepare me for it. She wants me to set a good example for my sisters, so they'll go to college, too."

"How old are your sisters?"

"Thirteen. They're twins and they were put on this earth to annoy me." He mixes his mac and cheese into his mashed potatoes and takes a bite. "That's actually why I was kind of a jerk that day at Dinosaur Valley. I was with my sisters and they were too focused on filming everything for their Snapchat that they didn't even listen to the cool story behind the dinosaur fossils. I had left them by the river and was taking a walk when I ran into you. Sorry about that."

"It's fine," I say. "I wasn't very nice either."

"Does this mean we're friends now?"

"It means we're not, *not* friends."

He stabs another hushpuppy. "Fair enough."

I guess Mason isn't too bad, at least when we're not in direct academic competition with each other. I can't believe I've known him for years but never knew he had twin sisters or that his mother was an immigrant. I see him twice a week at STEM Club and I know nothing about him. Maybe I should turn down the Ice Queen vibes just a tad.

"Where are your parents from?"

"Hmm?" he looks up.

"You said your mom didn't go to school here."

"She's from the Philippines. Dad is from Austin. They met at church when Dad was there visiting family. A few weeks later, they were married."

"My parents are from Stonebrook, but I'm sure you know

that. Everyone knows." I push and pull the tab on my Coke can until it breaks off. "My grandparents are from Stonebrook. And even my great grandparents are from Austin, which is still in Texas. We are the most boring family in the world."

"Is that why you're scared to go to Colorado?"

"I'm not scared," I say, pressing the soda tab between my finger and thumb. "It's just hard to break tradition. My whole family wants me to go to A&M."

"Nothing wrong with A&M." His eyes meet mine, and a coy smile tugs at his lips. "You know, for a basic white girl."

"Hey!" I throw my soda tab at him.

He catches it with an impressive flick of his wrist. "What are you doing later tonight?"

I swallow. The air in the room seems to have shifted over the last two seconds. I remember Maggie's insistence that I ask him on a date at Dinosaur Valley. But she didn't know our history... she was just being Maggie. Hopelessly optimistic and boy crazy. "I don't know," I say, remembering the robotics competition the whole club had wanted to attend. "Why?"

"You still going to the robotics thing? It promises to be an exciting deadly competition." He wiggles his eyebrows. "Deadly to robots, I mean. The only blood spilled will be oil. I promised Vu I'd have him on FaceTime so he can watch."

"Yeah, I'll probably stop by," I say. "Janise and Anna want pictures too."

"You want to go together?"

That's not exactly a date, I tell myself. So why does it make my heart speed up?

"Sure."

"Cool." He taps the table with his fingertips. "We'll make a game of it. Bet on which robot will win. The winner can get some kind of prize...like pizza."

"And the loser?" I say.

His lips move to the side of his mouth. "The loser has to accept her offer to FLU."

I roll my eyes. "You're not as funny as you think you are."

"Oh, Honey Blackwell," he says, standing and collecting our empty plates. "You have no idea how funny I think I am."

CHAPTER FIFTEEN

The rest of the day speeds by quicker than any day at school ever has. I sit in on lectures and workshops and fill two notebooks with notes. While it's all educational, it's so much more fun than regular high school work. It gives me a whole new outlook on college life.

The robot wars start at seven in the evening and last until midnight. I grab some pizza from the dinner buffet table and take it up to my hotel room to get ready for tonight. I wore jeans and a T-shirt today, but Mason dressed like a college student in comparison to me. He seemed so put together—so not himself. The Mason I saw today was the exact opposite of the Mason at school. That guy wears jeans and the same hoody almost every day and every word out of his mouth is something annoying or know-it-all. Even though we're just meeting up to watch robots rip each other to shreds, I want to be a better version of myself tonight, too. Tonight, we're future college students, not high school kids.

The large ballroom that held the keynote speech this

morning has been transformed for the robot wars. A stage is assembled in the middle of the room. It reminds me of a wrestling ring, except the walls are plexiglass instead of ropes. Each robot belongs to a team, and a dozen teams line up on one side of the room. Some teams have quite a following, with fans wearing shirts sporting their favorite robot. An announcer table is set up next to the stage, along with a projector screen that breaks down each robot match in brackets. Each member of tonight's winning team gets a ten-thousand-dollar scholarship.

All of the robots are on display right now, but I decide to wait outside the ballroom for Mason so we can see them together. Before we left lunch earlier, we'd agreed to meet up here right at seven. He arrives right on time with an easygoing smile on his face. His eyes sparkle when he sees me across the hallway. He hasn't changed clothes since earlier today. There's nothing wrong with his black button up shirt and jeans but it's making me regret my curled hair and sparkly tank top.

"You look pretty."

WHAT.

Mason's compliment is quick and easy, and he doesn't stare at me after he says it; he just falls into step with me. Maybe he doesn't even realize he said it, but I'm playing his words on repeat in my head as we walk into the ballroom.

Mason's hands shove in his pockets and stay there while we walk around the perimeter of the room. We stop and check out each robot, staying off to the side to let the diehard fans get up close. Some people take this stuff very seriously. It's like Comic Con, but for people obsessed with robotics.

"My money is on Sir Kill-a-lot," Mason says after we've made a trip around the room. "What about you?"

"That one looks vicious." I nod toward the aluminum robot featuring saws for hands. "But I think I'm rooting for Doomba."

"Solid choice," Mason says. "It's small, but powerful."

"And all that Kevlar should protect against Sir Kill-a-lot's saws."

"Shall we make a bet?"

"I don't have any money," I say. "And I am not betting on college admissions."

He snorts. "Money is the fool's currency, Honey Blackwell. Let's wager with information."

"I'm intrigued," I say.

On the projector screen, the first two robots are about to compete. Each robot has a team of five people who designed, built, and operate it. Both teams are carrying their robots toward the stage, flanked on all sides by adoring fans. Some people even brought homemade signs to wave in the air. Something tells me there's a whole world of robot fandom out there and this event is just scratching the surface.

"This match is between Megasaurous and Terabyte Titan," Mason says. "Which one are you betting on?"

"What's the wager?" I say.

"Winner has to agree with loser's opinions at the next STEM Club meeting."

"Oh, that'll be fun having you agree with me." I grin. "I'll bet on Megasaurous."

"Damn," he says, clicking his tongue. "I am totally going to lose."

We stand in the crowd, watching the projector screen for closeup footage of the robot war. There are too many people here to get a good view of the action up on stage. This first battle lasts only three minutes and twelve seconds, and Megasaurous wins.

I close my eyes and toss my head back, reveling in my win. "The next STEM Club meeting is going to be sweeeeeet."

"Yeah, yeah," Mason says, glancing at the screen which shows the next two robots about to battle. "Let's do best two out of three. I'm betting on Sir Kill-a-lot this time."

"What are we betting this time?"

"Loser gives the winner their phone number."

I cock an eyebrow. "That kind of sounds like the loser will still be the winner."

"Not really," Mason says. "The winner just has the loser's number. That doesn't mean they'll call them."

"You see me twice a week in STEM Club, what do you need my number for?"

Mason scoffs. "The question is what do YOU need my number for? Weirdo. You see me twice a week!"

"You are so confident for someone who has already lost one bet."

He shrugs. "What can I say? My luck tends to show up at the last minute."

"My contacts list is already pretty long, but I guess it can hold another number," I say, checking out the scoreboard. Both robots seem equally matched as far as their statistics go. "I'll take that bet."

"Great," Mason says. He reaches for his phone. "Let me just make some room for your number..."

"You freaking wish."

The next battle begins and we each cheer for our robot. This battle lasts for nine grueling minutes that actually make me start to feel sympathy for Sir Kill-a-lot, the hunk of metal that is absolutely getting pummeled by Ms. Chomp. The winner is declared and I turn to Mason, the cockiest grin imaginable on my face.

I pull out my phone and hand it to him. "Pay up."

He does this little half-grin thing with his lips and it makes my stomach flutter. I watch while he takes my phone and types in his phone number into a new contact. Mason isn't as tall as Luca. He's only a couple inches taller than I am, and I'm staring right at his lips. It occurs to me that the height difference would make it so very easy to just lean over and kiss him. Heat floods through my whole body. I can't believe I just thought that.

On my phone, Mason clicks on the new contact name and types *Mason (like the jar)*, and then saves it.

"The next battle starts soon," he says, rubbing his hands together. "I will win eventually."

"You sure about that? You seem to have zero luck."

He waves my words away. "Nah. I have luck. It just holds out on me...it'll show up."

"Well you better bet something good. I'm starting to feel bad for you. All this losing might harm your gigantic ego."

"My ego is perfectly normal-sized."

I roll my eyes. "The match is about to start. What are we betting?"

His bottom lip curls under his teeth while he looks at the scoreboard, then back to me. "If my luck has any chance of showing up, I need to bet something crazy. Something like... loser has to kiss the winner or something."

My smile fades. I suddenly feel all clumsy and out of place. My heart speeds up and I shift on my feet. This is *not* the Mason I go to school with. This is some other guy. Some cute guy, with a nice smile and banter that doesn't make me want to punch him in the face.

"Kidding," Mason says, taking a small step backward. "I was just playing around."

I fold my arms across my chest and glare at him. "Never gonna happen."

I know he was kidding. But why does he always seem to say exactly what I'm thinking? And why, at this very second, did my body decide to get all warm and tingly, my cheeks hot, my heart skippy like it's been shot right through the center with a metaphorical arrow?

The buzzer sounds and the battle begins. We're too late to make a bet on this one. The smell of motor oil overwhelms my senses and brings me back to reality, which is good because the last thing I need is to think of Mason in *that* way.

The robots clash and grind and battle it out. The air turns a bit hazy. The smell of burned rubber and oil makes me cover my face. On stage, one robot has smoke billowing out of one end. The crowd is loving every second of this massacre, even as crew members rush out with fire extinguishers in hand.

The large guy in front of me cheers and pumps his fist in the air. He gets so excited about the robot's demise that he stumbles backward, knocking into me, which makes me stumble backward. Mason puts an arm around my back, steadying me on my feet. His other hand grabs my shoulder, steering me to his left. "You'll get trampled over there," he says, stepping into the place where I was standing just a few seconds ago.

My skin warms from his touch. My spine tingles. It comes on so quickly I might lose my balance. I take a deep breath. This cannot be happening. I've waited all my life to feel this way about Luca. I've waited so long I thought maybe I was broken.

Now, of all times, my body decides to tell me in very vivid terms that it is not broken. That it has a huge crush on someone. Not just any guy, but Mason Ramos.

What the hell is happening?

CHAPTER SIXTEEN

I am so over driving long distances. It's just past eleven at night when I finally pull into my driveway after the second day of the conference. My legs feel numb and my hands hurt because I drove the whole four hours without stopping. I managed to be so busy all day that I never ran into Mason. That doesn't mean I wasn't thinking about him nonstop. I am so ready to be home so things can go back to normal and Mason can continue being Stonebrook High Mason not weirdly attractive and sweet STEM Conference Mason.

All I want to do is fall into bed—or maybe take a hot shower first—and sleep off the weekend. Unfortunately, my parents have other plans.

"How was the drive?" Mom asks when I walk through the door. She and Dad are both standing here as if they've been waiting at the front window ever since I texted them four hours ago that I was heading home.

"Tiring," I say over a yawn.

Dad gives me a quick hug. He's still in his work clothes,

the classic khaki pants and R&B polo. "So what did you learn at this fancy science weekend?"

"All kinds of things."

"Like?" He gives me one of those stares he reserves for summer interns who can't hack construction work.

"Science...stuff." I know I learned a lot this weekend; my laptop is filled with notes, pictures, and links to check out later. It's my dad's scrutinizing gaze that's making all that information catch on fire in my brain and evaporate from my memory.

"College stuff?" Mom asks, giving me a hopeful smile.

I nod. "I discovered that earth sciences are definitely my favorite. That's what I want to major in at FLU."

"You know what college has great earth science programs?" Dad says. "A&M."

I draw in a deep breath. "Can we please not talk about this now?"

"Blaine," Mom says softly. "It's a school night. Don't hound her about A&M."

"Did you know that working at the family business means you can write your own paychecks and be your own boss?" Dad says, completely ignoring Mom. The look he gives me is so infuriating. He's not mad. He's looking at me like I'm a little kid who just asked why the sky is blue. To him, I'm still his little girl, still this stupid kid with no idea about the real world. He thinks FLU is just a phase and that he knows best. I clench my hands into fists.

"I don't want to be a real estate agent."

Mom's head tilts. She looks as though I've just stabbed her in the back. And maybe I have.

Dad just shrugs. "So? We can hire more agents. There are plenty of places for you at R&B. You could start some earth-friendly recycled renovation line or buy into all that handmade furniture you're always taking about. You could do whatever you wanted if you stayed here and worked at the family company. Don't you get that?"

"Dad, I do want to work with you. But I want college, too. Why can't I take four years off to go to my dream school first?"

"Because it's a waste of money," Dad says. "The real world is harsh. Jobs are scarce and kids like you are drowning in student loan debt with no job prospects on the horizon. Why wouldn't you just stay here and prosper where you know you have a job? Do you realize how much hard work we put into building this company? And you just want to throw it away?"

I grit my teeth and let out a frustrated groan. There's no arguing with my dad when he gets like this. He became successful with hard work in his hometown. Maybe that's good enough for him, but it's not good enough for me.

"Just because my dreams aren't your dreams doesn't make them wrong."

Dad's nostrils flare. "Where did this sudden desire come from? Why do you want to run away from your life here?"

"I don't know." It's the best answer I can give because I've been asking myself this question for weeks. Things were fine. My life was good, graduation was approaching, and my future was set. Now I've screwed it all up with the possibility of doing something different. Luca and I are weird. My parents are mad at me. Why can't I just be the girl who is happy with what she has?

"That's *enough!*" Mom says with an intensity that cuts through Dad's tension. "Everyone go to bed."

She walks out of the room as calm as if she hadn't just yelled at us. The rising sting of tears burns in my eyes. I rush upstairs, leaving both my suitcase and all this drama in the foyer to be dealt with later. Mom was mistaken when she said it's a school night because tomorrow is a teacher in-service day, which means I can technically sleep in as late as I want. I brush my teeth and crawl into bed and try to recall all of that exhaustion I'd felt just an hour ago, but I am wide awake.

I can't help it. I text Luca.

Me: Parents pissing me off. You awake?

He doesn't reply until the next morning.

Luca: Now I am. Wanna come over?

CHAPTER SEVENTEEN

Luca's house is the mirror of my own house in floorplan only. Inside, his mom has decorated everything in this rustic, farmhouse style that's a huge contrast to my house's sleek black furniture and modern art. For being lifelong best friends, the moms have very different tastes. Even with their differences in décor, both houses equally feel like home to me.

"Coffee?" Luca says after meeting me on the back porch.

"No, thanks."

We head upstairs without talking. A few weeks ago, the silence wouldn't matter, but now it's a tiny bit awkward. I don't know what I expect to see in his bedroom. I haven't been up here since we broke up, and it feels like it'll be as different as everything else in my life. But Luca's bedroom is exactly the same. Neatly made bed in the middle of the room, TV mounted on the wall with a stack of video games tumbling on the floor below it. Dirty clothes mostly tossed in the hamper in his closet. Pictures of us everywhere.

I touch a photo of us from last year's R&B Halloween party. Maggie had painted our faces to look like sugar skulls and she did such a great job you can hardly tell that it's us in the photo. Of course I'd recognize Luca's azure eyes anywhere. That was a fun night. It's hard to imagine going to work parties—or any party—with someone who isn't Luca.

Mason enters my mind. Would he be fun at parties? Would he go along with whatever silly couples costume idea I wanted?

Luca turns on the soundbar under his TV and connects his phone to it. Music fills the air, a steady thump of bass that will ensure our conversation isn't overheard by anyone.

He sits on his bed, watching me. His broad shoulders seem even bigger after a weekend apart. Has he been hitting the gym hard now that we don't spend as much time together? Is it boredom workouts or is he trying to attract other girls? Once again, I think about Mason, and wonder if Luca has a girl he thinks about the same way. My heart gets this little pinch of jealousy.

This is what I wanted, I tell myself.

"So how was the conference?" Luca asks.

I sit facing him at the foot of his bed, crossing my legs so that our knees are touching. "I don't want to talk about that."

"Was it that bad?"

"No, it was fun."

He looks down at his lap. "So you're still wanting to accept that college, huh?"

"Yes."

His jaw clenches as he taps his fingers on my knees. "Why do you want to leave me for four years?"

"I don't want to leave you. I want to go college."

"And yet it's exactly the same thing." He shakes his head. "Why can't you just go to college here?"

I shrug off his question with a playful smirk. "I saw your

Snapchat feed this morning. Was that cute blonde girl your hot date this weekend?"

His head jerks back and he gags. "That *cute blonde girl* is my cousin."

I sit up and glare at him. "What cousin? I know your entire family."

"Yes…" he says, tapping his palms on my knees. "And you know my uncle Trent who recently found out he has a kid from his college girlfriend? That's her."

"Wow," I say. It was just last Christmas when Uncle Trent told us about his newfound teenage daughter. "And now y'all are hanging out at beach parties? Damn, how long have we been broken up?"

He laughs. "I met her last night. She goes to Apple Valley High but she just started dating Raymond Sosa. She wants to meet you."

I smack my hands on top of his which are still on my knees while I sit cross-legged on his bed. "So how many dates are you at now?"

"Three. You?"

"Still just two," I say, covering my face with my hands. "I am such a loser."

"Nah, you're just the tortoise and I'm the hare."

"Wow." I drag my hands down my face. "Could you be lamer?"

He grins. "Were your two dates fun?"

I shrug. "Yeah, I guess. I think I might be going about it the wrong way… I said yes to Chase but I didn't really like him. It's like I'm desperately trying to find five people to date quickly to get it over with."

"So?"

"That feels like the wrong way."

"It's what I'm doing," Luca says. The music stops for a second as his phone vibrates, but he ignores it. That's another trait that my friends are always so jealous of. Other guys are on their phones constantly, but Luca doesn't interrupt our quality time for some random text.

My friends act like it's some ultra-rare thing that my boyfriend isn't glued to his phone. They think I'm *sooo* lucky. But now that I think about it, I didn't see Mason's phone the entire time we hung out at the convention, except for when he Facetimed Vu during the last half of the robot wars. I rarely ever see it during STEM Club either. Luca isn't the only guy in the world with good manners.

Ugh, Honey. Why are you thinking about Mason?

Luca takes a deep breath and then falls backward on his bed, his hands tucking under his head. The song changes. An old indie rock tune plays, and I'm thrown back to junior high where Luca and I listened to a Zombie Radio album nonstop for months. I shift on my knees and then lay down next to him on my side, my elbow holding up my head.

"I love this song."

He nods. "It always reminds me of you. Like that time you requested it at the skating rink and we tried to hold hands and skate and it did not work out well."

I chuckle at the memory. "Why do all the movies make holding hands and skating look romantic? It's impossible to hold hands and not fall."

"We were dumb kids," he says, staring at his ceiling. "We didn't know anything about romance."

"Do we know anything about it now?" I ask.

"Apparently not." Luca turns toward me. "I took one of my dates to that skating rink and it was a total disaster."

"Did you try holding hands with her? You know that's a recipe for getting a face full of floor."

He laughs. "No... no hand holding. But apparently she had never skated before, so it was like trying to teach a toddler how to walk."

"Sexy," I say, wiggling my eyebrows.

Luca's smirk is so perfectly him. I can't imagine that look on any other guy. And yet... Mason's smirk was pretty damn cute too.

Luca turns to me, propping his head up on his elbow. "The sooner we get through these dates, the sooner you'll realize we're soulmates."

I breathe in slowly, concentrating on not rolling my eyes. "You really still think we're soulmates?"

"Of course," he says. "A few random dates aren't going to change that."

The music glitches several more times as Luca's phone lights up with more texts. "You going to answer that?" I say, nodding toward the phone he left next to the sound bar.

He shrugs. "I'll get it later."

"Who even texts you that much?"

"Some girls are having a hard time only getting one date," he says sheepishly. "Lesson learned. I'm not giving anyone my number from now on."

A little stab of jealousy pierces into me. Am I jealous because girls like Luca? Or because I haven't gotten the guts to text Mason yet?

"You should at least reply and tell them you're not interested."

"Trust me, I have." Luca exhales and runs a hand over his weary face. "Dating is exhausting."

"You seem to be good at it."

"Duh." He clicks his tongue. "I'm good at everything."

I punch him in the arm.

There's a quick *tap tap tap* on Luca's door, which is Jill's callsign for when she's about to barge in on us. Of all the parents, she's the only one who tries *not* to catch us making out. "Come in," Luca calls out.

Jill is all smiles as she enters the room wearing black leggings, running shoes, and a baggy hot pink workout shirt. Workout clothes are her favorite outfit to wear when she's doing anything but actually working out.

"Hey, kiddos," she says, all smiles like usual. "How was Houston, Honey?"

"Academic," I say. "I learned so much. It was fun."

"You're so smart, Honey. I'm proud of you."

"She is smart," Luca says, glancing at me. "Smarter than the rest of us."

Jill nods. "We are lucky to have her."

"If I'm so smart do you think I'd be better off at Fault Line University?"

Luca's gaze pierces into me. He's not angry. He's... contemplative.

"Oh?" Jill leans against the doorframe. "You're still considering that school?"

Pain slices through the inside of my lip before I realize I'm biting it. "Maybe..." I say, glancing at Luca. He's gone completely still. "My parents think it's a stupid idea."

Jill's brows wrinkle. "Why?"

"If I go to college, I can't work at R&B."

When Jill scoffs, she looks like her son. Both of their foreheads crease in exactly the same spot. "R&B isn't some magical place that disappears if you go to college for a few years." She reaches over and squeezes my knee. "If you want to go to that college, then go to that college. We'll support you."

The music skips again, and this time Luca gets up and checks his phone. I guess I can't blame him, he's been sitting here rigid, staring at the floor while his mom and I discuss a subject he's not too happy about.

I stand up and hug Jill, because even if college talk annoys Luca, it's still important to me. "Sometimes I wish you were my mom and that Luca got stuck with my parents."

"We don't have to be blood to be family." She holds me out at arms' length and gives me a satisfied smile, her eyes crinkling in the corners as she looks at me. "Besides, one day I'll be your mother-in-law, and that's close enough."

Luca lowers his phone, his gaze shooting straight to me. I'm supposed to agree with her, just like I have every single time the subject of our future comes up. It's not a question, or a possibility in this family. It's a certainty that Luca Rollins and Honey Blackwell will get married someday.

She knows it. Luca knows it. My parents know it.

I'm the only one who thinks it might be a bad idea.

CHAPTER EIGHTEEN

Our next STEM Club meeting has gone back to the bring-your-own-lunch type of meeting that it was before Anna's free gift ended up giving most of the club free gifts for the entire weekend. My science friends spend the first several minutes of the meeting discussing how sick everyone got and how long it took to feel normal again. The empty science lab echoes with laughter and I wonder if I'll ever find another group of nerds like this after high school is over.

I chew on my garden salad and scan over the dozen internet tabs that are open on my school laptop. Maggie has only found the one expensive copy of her book on eBay, but I'm hoping if I just dig deep enough on the World Wide Web I'll find another copy somewhere else. A cheaper copy. Surely more than one of these things were printed.

Usually our club meetings are conducted more professionally, but with just a few weeks of school left, the STEM conference was our big finale for the year, and now our club is in goof-off mode. Technically, I'm the secretary and I should be taking notes, but there's no reason to document the rest of the group's food poisoning tales, so I'm slacking off and researching this book for Maggie. If I can somehow get her a copy, I'll go down in history as the *best*, best friend ever.

"It's kind of ironic that the two club members who can't stand each other are the two who went to the conference," Anna says. She chuckles over a bite of her sandwich. "I'm surprised you didn't rip each other's heads off."

I glance up, having been brought into the conversation once I heard my name. Mason sits at the far end of the table, kicked back with his feet on the table as always. He's also on his school computer so I can only see his brows over the top of the screen. We're not allowed to decorate these school-issued laptops, but that hasn't stopped Mason from fixing a NASA sticker to his.

"We barely saw each other," I say. "It was a really busy weekend." A tingle shoots down my spine. I figured everything would go back to normal once we were back in school, and that the Mason I'd semi-flirted with in Houston would not be flirt-worthy now that we're back here. Still, it's a painful realization that my assumptions were correct. Mason hasn't looked at me or talked to me all week in computer programming class. He wears his Air pods all day like the broody weirdo he is.

"Forget about Mason," Anna says. She sits directly across from me and reaches out the hand that's not holding her sandwich. Her fingers close around my wrist and she makes some serious eye contact. "How many hot guys did you flirt with in Houston?"

Just one, I think. *And he's currently ignoring me.*

"None," I say.

Anna's jaw drops. "Seriously? Did you flirt with *anyone*?"

I shake my head.

"Come on now, I thought we decided Honey's love life wasn't STEM Club material," Janise says. "We only have a few weeks until graduation and we should probably figure out our freshman recruitment plan."

"Yes," I say with an enthusiastic nod. "Let's talk about that."

Vu raises his hand. He is the only person in our club who does that.

"Yes, Vu?" Janise says. I think she secretly loves feeling like an authority figure.

"I know this is everyone else's senior year but I think the club should invest in a robot next year," he says. "The robot competition was so cool. They actually broadcasted it live online so I watched it between episodes of vomiting. You can get scholarships from winning competitions, so I bet we can convince our school to allow it."

"I agree," Janise says. She writes something in her notebook and I drop my fork to type up Vu's idea in my meeting notes for the day. Janise grins. "We should make this our final project for the year. Our legacy will be leaving the funds and the plan for a robot to the next year of STEM Club."

"Ooh!" Anna says, snapping her fingers. "This can be a great way to recruit new members during summer freshman orientation! We'll promise them a robot."

"This is a great idea," I say, nodding at Vu. "We can start calling around for sponsors."

"What about R&B Construction?" Anna asks me. "You think your dad would sponsor it?"

"Maybe." A lump rises in my throat at the thought of asking him. Dad isn't exactly happy with me now so donating to a STEM Club is probably not high on his list.

"I'll put R&B down as a 'maybe'," Janise says, writing

more notes. She points the tip of her pen at our youngest member. "Vu, it's up to you and the robot to keep this little club alive."

He puts a hand across his heart. "Even if I'm the only member, this club will live on."

"Mason?" Janise leans forward on the black science table to see him. "You going to weigh in today?"

Mason sits at the far edge of the table, tapping a mechanical pencil on his keyboard. He blinks. My stomach tenses.

"Sorry," he says, clearing his throat. "My mind was elsewhere."

"Your mind belongs to me twice a week for thirty five minutes," Janise says with a click of her tongue. "You cool with the robot legacy?"

"Very cool with the robot legacy," he says, twisting the pencil in his fingers. He glances up and our eyes meet. I don't know why, but I smile. He looks away.

Janise heaves a sigh. "I get it, guys. Senior Slump is in full effect and we're all lazy, but we have one last project to go. We owe it to our little Junior here," she says, reaching over and ruffling Vu's hair. He rolls his eyes. "Let's get a list of ten businesses to ask for sponsorship before lunch is over. Anna, you can write the proposal for Principal Baker and Honey will edit it. Vu, Mason, you two do some research and figure out what it'll cost for a robot."

Just like that, our lazy meeting is over. I type quickly, keeping track of everything Janise said. Anna and I brainstorm on our proposal idea. After four years, we know how to word something in a way that will convince Mr. Baker to approve it. It feels good having something to keep me busy, which is probably why I've been obsessing over finding another copy of

Maggie's book lately. When my brain goes idle, it thinks of Mason. I'm having a hard time processing that.

Me? Mason? Nope. My brain just won't compute it. And now that I'm thinking about it, my cheeks burn, and I have to focus on my conversation with Anna so my thoughts don't trail back to that night in Houston. What would have happened if I agreed to Mason's final bet? My cheeks feel warm until the bell rings and I head out into the hallway for some fresh air.

"Honey, wait up," Vu says, jogging a bit to catch up with me.

"What's up?" I say, peering down. If I'm a little short for my age, he's very short for his age.

He leans in a bit, eyes darting around to clear the way before speaking. "You know Mason has a huge crush on you, right?"

"Huh?" The sound that comes out of me is more like a garbled noise than a coherent word. "What are you talking about?"

Vu hitches his backpack up on his shoulders, pressing his lips flat while we walk. "I know I probably shouldn't tell you —I mean, I always thought it was obvious, but clearly you're clueless."

I try to speak, but only an indignant huff of hair comes out. I take a deep breath. "There's no way that's true. Mason and I are enemies."

"Yeah, right. You're pretend enemies." Vu snorts. "That's only the oldest plotline in every story ever!"

"Has it ever occurred to you that Mason and I seem like enemies because we *are* enemies?"

"Oh yeah?" Vu says. "Then explain to me why he's all sad

that he gave you his number a week ago and you never reached out to him?"

The warmth in my cheeks is back again. "How do you know about that?"

"We're friends. He told me he had a crush on you way back in fifth grade when we were at science camp together." Vu's lips slide to the side of his mouth. "I guess he's carried a torch for you all this time."

We're still walking down Stonebrook High's main corridor, though now I've forgotten what classroom I'm supposed to be in when the next bell rings.

"Thanks for telling me," I say, stopping near the vending machines. If I keep walking I'll end up in the locker rooms and there's never been a reason for me to be in the athletic part of the school without Luca.

He touches my arm. "Please don't tell him I said anything."

"If I don't have the guts to text him, I definitely won't have the guts to tell him you told me that," I mutter.

Vu's sneakers squeak on the shiny tile floor as he turns back around. His face breaks into a huge, toothy grin. "You like him too?"

I roll my eyes. "I am not answering that question."

He gives me a knowing nod. "I think you just did."

CHAPTER NINETEEN

Stonebrook's public library is literally an old house that is full of books that might have been useful several decades ago. The house was donated to the historical foundation way before I was even born, and people filled it up with old, dusty, gross books and called it a library. It is *not* a library. My parents think it's part of the charm of living in a small Texas town. I think there's nothing charming about driving forty-five minutes to the next town every time we need something that's not available in Stonebrook.

I don't mind the drive today, because I'm on a secret mission of friendship.

Maggie has been especially down lately because she can't afford the rare Egyptian makeup book and I hate seeing her so gloomy. And now my brain is ten kinds of jacked up with the bombshell Vu dropped on me after lunch. My heart has been beating fast all day. I didn't want to chance embarrassing myself in front of Mason in our computer programming class, so I spent the entire period on my computer, looking for the Egyptian makeup book.

My desperation yielded results. The Apple Valley Library in the next town over has a copy. I can't check it out since I'm not a member of the library, and the only way to be a member is to live in the city limits. My plan is to find it, Xerox every page, and then give it to Maggie. It'll be a thank you gift to show her how much I love her, especially since she's dedicated all of our time together to helping me solve this college/Luca problem.

Daydreams of how awesome I am fill my thoughts as I drive Mom's car to the large modern building that looks exactly like what a library should look like, because Apple Valley values usefulness over small town charm. I have thought of a dozen fun ways to present Maggie this book, and I can't wait to get my hands on it.

Inside, the chill of the air conditioning is a stark contrast to the warm summer air outside. The smell of books reminds me of my childhood when the moms would bring Luca and me here for story time once a month. Apple Valley's library has a vast children's section that's decorated with colorful paper-mâché versions of picture book characters. A large hungry caterpillar hangs from the ceiling, and a Clifford the big red dog sits next to a large window.

I head toward the non-fiction books, scanning the callsigns on the aisles until I find the one that matches what I've scribbled on the back of my hand from the library's website. My heart races in anticipation. Maybe I should have brought Maggie with me so she could experience the excitement of looking for it, but this way she'll be surprised. Plus, this is a library and you have to be quiet. When it comes to Maggie's passion about makeup artistry, she's never very quiet about it.

The author's last name is Zogby, so I kneel down on the carpeted flooring in search of the treasure of this rare book.

And there it is. Carefully, as if it might fall apart if it discovers how valuable it is, I pull the hardback book from the shelf. It's a little shelf-worn on the edges, but it's real. And the cover matches the one online. It's printed by an independent publisher that went out of business decades ago. This is it.

I grin and do a little dance as I stand up, turning the pages to look at the glossy photos within. Maggie is going to freak. I bounce on the balls of my feet, clutching the book to my chest. Everything has felt like a gigantic loss lately, but this feels like a win.

"That must be a good book."

I startle, looking down the aisle but finding it empty. I turn the other way, and don't see anyone. The voice was whispered, so maybe I just imagined it. Then I see him. Staring at me through the large crack in the aisle of books in front of me. He's about my age, a Black guy with a dazzling grin, wearing an Apple Valley Student Council shirt.

"Sorry," he whispers. "I wasn't spying on you or anything. The dancing caught my attention."

"It is a good book," I say, feeling like I've been smacked on the head with a big dose of humiliation. What kind of weirdo dances in the library? I walk quickly away, toward the front of the library to the copy machine.

I put the book on the glass, cover down, because this gift to Maggie needs to be thorough. I want to copy every page, from the front cover to the back so it'll be almost as good as having the actual book until she can afford to buy her own copy. After lowering the lid, I press the green copy button.

Nothing happens.

I press it again. Still nothing.

I lift the lid and reposition the book as if that will somehow help. The tiny black and white digital screen just says *ready*. I give all the buttons a once-over, seeing if there's anything I'm missing here. I've made copies before at other places, and it's pretty easy. You just press the stupid green button.

After three more unsuccessful button presses, the screen goes from *ready* to *error 5003*.

"What the crap," I whisper in frustration. Glancing around, I see that the front desk is still empty. I'm not sure they'd be any help since the sign on the wall clearly states the copier is for library members only. If someone asks for my nonexistent library card, I'm screwed.

An evil thought crosses my mind. I could just steal the book. Walk right on out of here and never look back. But I can't do something like that. I've never so much as littered a piece of gum on the ground. I can't steal a book from the library, which is the one place that provides free entertainment for thousands of people. To be perfectly honest, making this copy is giving me ultra-guilty vibes, but I'm promising myself it's just temporary until Maggie and I can buy our own copy.

So no, I won't steal the real book. But... I *could* stash it in my purse, find a print store nearby and then discreetly bring the book back...

The guy who saw me dancing like an idiot is suddenly next to me, a half-grin on his lips as he watches my struggle with this machine.

"I think I know what the problem is," he says softly, in a perfect library whisper.

"Can you help?" I whisper back.

He nods. "See, the problem is you were trying to get this thing to make copies. But, unfortunately it's just a large ugly paperweight." He taps the paper tray, then rests his elbows on the top of it, then continues to whisper. "It hasn't worked right in years. The only thing this baby is good for is leaning against while you're talking with someone."

I hold back a laugh in an effort to stay quiet. "Well, in that case, this paperweight is doing a stellar job. But I need a machine that does a different job. One that actually makes copies."

"There's a teacher supply store close by and they have copiers and laminators and stuff."

Heaving a sigh, I pull out the book from the broken copier. "I don't have a library card, so I can't check it out and take it anywhere."

"I have a library card," he says, reaching out a hand.

I give him the book and feel a little stab of anxiety as it leaves my possession. I've come so close and I really don't want to miss out on getting this for Maggie. But the cute student council guy motions for me to follow him as he walks up to the self-checkout kiosk and scans his library card, then scans the barcode on the book. His name pops up on the screen: Brock Myers.

"My name is Honey, by the way."

"Brock," he says, flashing me a grin. "Nice to meet you."

A few seconds later, the computer confirms Brock is borrowing this book, and the transaction is complete. We didn't even need the librarian. I can't imagine Stonebrook's library ever upgrading to a thing like this. We still have a little old lady working the front counter, taking a very long time to hand stamp each book you want to check out.

"The teacher supply store is just down the block," he whispers, handing me back the book. "We can walk to it."

As soon as we're outside, I drop the soft whisper voice and speak normally. "Thanks for this." The warm sun is a welcome change from the cold library, but it makes me squint as I look up at my new library friend. "This is a huge help. Thank you."

"I have to confess that my intentions aren't just about being a good Samaritan," Brock says, stepping over a crack in the sidewalk.

I peer up at him. "What kind of ulterior motive could you have by checking out a book for me?"

"I… well…" His smile turns sheepish. "Any girl who dances in a library is a girl I'd like to ask on a date."

"Oh."

He tugs on the collar of his shirt, nervously clearing his throat. "That's not exactly the reaction I was hoping for," he says with a forced chuckle. "It's no big deal. I mean, I'd like to lie and say this StuCo shirt isn't mine so you'd think I'm cooler than I am but—"

"That wasn't a bad reaction," I say quickly, hoping to swiftly wash away his anxieties. He's totally cute and I don't want him thinking he's not attractive. "I was just surprised."

So surprised that it feels like some kind of lost-cause serendipity. Where was all this attention over the past couple of years? Here I thought finding five dates in five weeks would be a challenge I could only complete if I signed up for some shady dating service, but now this is the second time a guy I just met has flirted with me.

I smile up at Brock and he gives me a tentative smile back, and something dawns on me. It's not that I suddenly became desirable enough for random guys to like me. It's that for once in my whole life, I'm out here, living and doing and being myself without having Luca right by my side, proactively claiming me as his girlfriend.

"So…" Brock says, swaying his arms as we walk. "Does

this mean I should ask you on a date? Coffee at the shop across the street?"

"I'd like that," I say, thinking of Luca's phone and his constant text messages. I want to go on this date, but I don't want to lead Brock on. I still have two more dates after this one to accomplish. "I'm moving out of state for college in the fall so I can't really... get too involved with anyone right now."

"Gotcha." Brock stops and I realize we've walked all the way to the teacher supply store. He pulls open the door for me. "I'm heading to Caltech in the fall so I guess I'm in the same boat. But coffee is just coffee, right?"

I grin, mentally checking off the box for date number three in my head. "Coffee is just coffee."

CHAPTER TWENTY

"You had another date and waited until midnight to tell me?" My best friend's accent gets so much more pronounced when she's mad at me. She also gets a teensy bit hyperbolic. I check the time on my phone.

"It's not even eight-thirty!"

I can practically feel her eyes roll to the back of her skull. "It's still late. You should have called me the second the date ended to give me all the glorious details."

"Maybe I should have just FaceTimed you and propped up my phone in the middle of the date so you could be a part of it."

"Now that is forward thinking, Honey. I'm impressed."

I peel off a little star sticker and press it to the calendar on the wall above my desk. It's the third sticker I've added to the calendar. The third date. Two more to go.

"So...?" Maggie says. "I need all the details about this mystery Apple Valley man."

I stare at the photo of Luca and me at prom. It was taken just over a month ago, right after we won Cutest Couple, and

161

before my well-laid plans for the future suddenly cracked apart in the middle. It's framed and in a place of honor on the wall, since most of the photos around it are just stuck to the drywall with washi tape. Jill gave me that frame. If you strip away the professional makeup Maggie applied and the hair style and the fancy purple sequined dress, I know I look just the same now as I did in that photo, but I feel different. Older. Not necessarily wiser, but *something*.

"I don't know what you want me to say," I tell Maggie as I drag my gaze away from the prom photo, choosing to focus on the partially stolen handmade gift I made for her today. This is one of the reasons I can't tell her all the date details because I'd have to lie about why I was at the library. "He was cute and smart and nice, but we agreed we didn't want a relationship. We just had coffee."

"Blah. So no fireworks?"

"Nope. I didn't see any fireworks," I say with a sigh.

Maggie snorts. "You don't *see* fireworks, Honey. You *feel* them."

I run my hand over the smooth laminated paper of the gift she doesn't know exists yet. "How exactly do you feel a firework? That sounds painful."

"I swear, you are trying to be difficult," she says in a voice that's eerily like her own mom. "Obviously it's a metaphor. You feel the fireworks in your toes and your stomach and your… you know."

I laugh. "This conversation is taking a weird turn."

"I'm being serious. The fireworks are real, and I'm guessing you didn't feel them with this hot coffee guy."

"The only thing I felt with Brock was this weird pride that he thought I was good enough to ask on a date."

"That's a start… but it's not enough."

"He's going away to college in the fall so we both knew there was no point to the date. No one wants to start something that's about to end."

"That's a shite way of looking at it," she says. "True love doesn't care about colleges or long distance. True love finds a away. If he was really your soulmate, the second you met him you'd know it, and you would have done anything to be with him."

"I think you've been reading too many romance novels."

She scoffs. "Maybe you haven't been reading enough."

I scoff right back at her. "Is this the same Maggie Sinclair that went to the Women's March with me last year?"

"You can be a feminist and a hopeless romantic at the same time," she says with a profoundness in her tone that tells me I might have been a little too mean to her just now.

"I guess you're right."

"Always," Maggie chirps. "Ah, bullocks. Mum's yelling my name. I gotta go."

We hang up and I sit here contemplating, well, everything. Luca must be busy with work, the track team, and dating because he rarely ever texts me anymore and I never see him at school since I ride with Maggie and sit with her at lunch. At work, he's always on site helping with remodels, so I haven't seen him around the office.

Without anything to distract me, I am once again remembering that unexpected conversation with Vu. My brain zooms in on all thoughts of Mason, like he's an organism that's been slapped under a slide and I can't adjust the microscope to pan out and think of anything else but him.

The top stair in my house always creaks when someone steps on it, and I hear that sound now. I look up from my bed and squint at the hallway. My mom slips into the guest bedroom without looking my way. A few seconds later, the glow of the television fills the darkness. I get up and close my door, reminding myself to ask what show she's so obsessed with. I bet it's good if she's staying up late to watch it almost every night.

I have to know if Vu was telling the truth. While my incisors dig into my bottom lip, I search for Mason's number in my phone.

> **Me:** Yo
> **Mason (like the jar):** Honey?
> **Me:** How'd you know?
> **Mason (like the jar):** I haven't given my
>   number to anyone else lately. What's up?

Vu told me you have a crush on me. Is that true?

My thumbs hover over the screen. I have it all typed up. Just one tap of a button would send it.

I erase the text.

Maybe I don't need to be so obvious. Instead of ripping off the bandage, I'll play it cool and see if he reveals his feelings toward me in a more subtle way.

> **Me:** I'm still debating between FLU and A&M.
>   What made you choose FLU?
> **Mason (like the jar):** The college fair at school,
>   freshman year. I saw an FLU brochure and
>   immediately knew I wanted to go there. It's
>   the only college I applied to.
> **Me:** Wow. The college fair is why I chose to
>   apply to FLU, too. But it wasn't until this
>   year. I've always thought I would go to A&M.

> **Mason (like the jar):** Do you *want* to go to
> A&M?
> **Me:** I am ambivalent about A&M.
> **Mason (like the jar):** So accept FLU.
> **Me:** But college should be practical, not
> emotional. A&M is close and my parents are
> paying for it. They'll pay tuition but not
> room & board at FLU.

He doesn't reply right away. I sit here on my bed staring at my phone as my red blood cells replace themselves with anxiety. Why is he taking so long to reply? Is this what my friends feel like when they're waiting on a guy to text back? No wonder they complain so much.

If Mason really likes me, he'll find a way to say it.

My phone vibrates.

> **Mason (like the jar):** Don't let money be what
> stops you.

He sends an image of several papers laid out on his bed. They're scholarships, all awarded to Mason Ramos.

> **Mason (like the jar):** Joke's on you, student
> loans. I only need you for 99.999% of my
> college tuition now!

I grin and look back at the picture. He's been awarded at least a dozen small scholarships ranging in value from $250 to $1000.

> **Me:** That looks like it took so much work.

Mason (like the jar): I have now written
personal essays so many times I could recite
them from memory.
Me: Blah. I'd rather write about anything but
myself.
Mason (like the jar): write about how you
broke away from family tradition and
followed your own path in life.

I read his text several times. I hate that he knows me so well and I don't know him at all. With just that one text, he's summed up my life and my fear and the very thing preventing me from making a choice about my future.

My phone rings. It's a video call. My whole body goes cold and I leap off my bed and stare into the vanity mirror, taking stock of my post-shower, pre-hair-brushing appearance. I've got nothing attractive going on right now, but the only light in my room is from a lamp in the corner, so maybe he won't be able to tell. I could just let it go to voicemail but that might be more awkward than answering, so I take a deep breath and answer the damn phone.

Mason's face appears on the screen. His room is dark too, making his tanned skin seem paler in the dim glow of his television. His hair is all over the place.

"Hello," I say.

"So what's really going on?"

I sit a little straighter to hide that god-awful double chin look. "Huh?"

My insides cringe so hard. *Huh?* What kind of inarticulate single-cell organism have I been reduced to? So what if Mason is actually super cute when I think about it, and so what if he might have a crush on me and I might have a crush on him, too? I can't suddenly go all lovesick mumbling idiot around him. He's my mortal enemy.

At least until he tells me differently.

Mason gives me that serious look of his. "You don't need my opinion, Honey. I bet you don't even care about my opinion. So why ask what I think?"

"That's... not entirely true," I say, looking into the dark pixels of his eyes. "Maybe the fact that I don't care about your opinion is what makes your opinion important. You tell it like it is. You always have, and I respect that."

I swallow. *Please, please* say something, *anything* I can consider an admission of a crush. Even the slightest smile right now would convince me.

Mason sets the phone down in front of him, then opens his laptop. "If money's an issue, I have Sarika from the financial aid department on speed dial. I can help you get all that sorted out and we can start writing essays to get you some badass low dollar scholarships. I'll email you the easy ones right now."

"It's not the money, Mason. It's everything else."

"Everything else?" His eyes are on his computer screen. "You mean your boyfriend?"

My breath hitches. "Luca and I are broken up."

"Riiiight," he says. He types something into his laptop, then closes the lid and looks at me. "If you were actually broken up, you'd have accepted FLU by now."

A new email notification from Mason pops up on my phone and I swipe it away.

"That's not true," I say defensively.

"It is true." He gives a derisive little laugh. "You can blame your parents, or money, or whatever makes you sleep better, but if you made your own decisions without him, you'd be going to FLU."

My nostrils flare. "You know nothing about me and Luca."

He rolls his eyes. "I know you go to all of his track meets but he's never been to a STEM Club meeting. I know you sit with his friends at lunch but he doesn't ever hang out with you and Maggie. I know you decorate his locker for Valentine's day, and his birthday, and Christmas, but he doesn't do anything to yours."

"That's because guys don't do that stuff—"

"A guy who really loved you would do all those things."

"Like you know anything about love," I snap. We've fallen right back into our normal bickering routine. It's almost comforting to replace my nerves with annoyance.

Mason leans back against his headboard, one hand holding the phone in front of him and the other one resting behind his head. "You do know May first is in two days, right?"

"Yeah, I know."

"Okay, next question. You know the final day to accept FLU is *also* on May first?"

I roll my eyes. "Of course I know that."

He clicks his tongue. "Tick tock, Honey. You can make yourself happy, or you can make everyone else happy." He brings the phone a little closer to his face. For just a moment, he's STEM Convention Mason again. "Just make sure he would make the same sacrifices for you before you sacrifice everything for him."

CHAPTER TWENTY-ONE

Tears stream down Maggie's face. She tries to blink them away but they just roll down her cheeks and sparkle in the sunlight. In my lap, our to-go box of cafeteria pizza is so hot it's making my legs sweat through my leggings. Eating lunch outside had seemed like a great idea, but it's almost too hot to justify the break from our fluorescent white-walled school.

Maggie clutches the Xeroxed book to her chest, closes her eyes, and tilts her head back to the sky. "You are my favorite friend ever." She says each word like it's its own sentence. I smile to myself. Mission accomplished.

"I know it's not the real thing but, at least you can read the text and stuff."

"Are you kidding?" She holds it out and admires the laminated pages, which I also had spiral bound with a hard plastic cover at the teacher supply store. "It's perfect. Makeup Maria's subscribers will all be flocking to my channel now."

She twists her dark curly locks into a bun at the top of her head, securing it with a chopstick. "I can't wait to get my silver play button before she gets one and I'm going to hang that sucker in my booth at school."

I shift the hot pizza onto the bench space between us. "I can't believe we only have five months left until you go to New York."

"You mean *four* months," Maggie says, her gaze on the book in her hands.

Maggie decided to attend makeup school in NYC over a year ago. It's expensive, but she has an aunt who lives in Brooklyn and is letting her live there for free while she attends the intensive six month makeup artistry program. I plan on visiting her every time I can save up enough money for a plane ticket to New York. Ever since she snagged a coveted spot at that school, we've counted off the months remaining until she goes on to pursue her dream. That's how I know she's wrong.

"It's five months until September."

She nods. "Yes, but Fault Line University starts in August, so you'll be leaving a month sooner than I will."

I am so not in the mood to get into another college argument with her. Between Maggie, and Mason, and Aunt Bree demanding that I go to FLU, and Luca and my parents begging me not to, I'm sore from being pulled in opposite directions. The pros and cons are too evenly matched. My future is a perfectly balanced libra scale that refuses to tip in one direction.

I heave a relenting sigh and say, "Five months if I don't go, four months if I do go."

My non-committal answer must be sufficient because Maggie simply nods while she eats. She picks off a stray olive from her pizza slice and tosses it to the ground behind her.

We eat in silence for a while, sitting out here baking in the sun while a few other students hang out on nearby picnic tables and benches. Some soccer players kick a ball around behind us. Tonight is Decision Day, the final date to accept or deny my college acceptance to FLU. I have to log in and accept or deny my dream college before midnight. I keep telling myself I'll wait until tonight before I make my choice, but deep down, where all the secret parts of my soul reside, I already know the truth.

I won't be accepting Fault Line University.

It doesn't matter how often I daydream about the Colorado mountains and the idea of packing up and leaving this small town, I just know I won't do it. I can't annoy my parents and break Luca's heart and go off and do something totally unnecessary. I want to. I want it more than anything. Just because you want something doesn't mean it's right.

My phone vibrates on the bench beside me. I finish my slice of pizza before looking over at it, and immediately wish I had dropped everything to check it five minutes ago.

Mason's name (and his little parenthetical joke) are on my phone screen. Maggie sees it and lifts a brow. "I thought you didn't like him," she says in her sarcastic you're-a-big-liar voice.

"It's probably a STEM Club thing," I say, clicking his message.

> **Mason (like the jar):** My history teacher loves
> me and has given me two VIP tickets to the
> LMSN Crystals of India exhibit which techni-
> cally closed yesterday but extra important
> people like myself can explore it tonight
> before they take it all away.

Maggie waves her hands at me. "Well? What's it say?"

"I'm not sure. I think he's bragging about museum tickets."

I show her the text. She slaps my arm. "No, dummy. He's inviting you. Wait... oh my gosh—is this a date? Is he asking you on a date?"

"No part of that text is a date invitation."

My phone vibrates again.

Mason (like the jar): Are you free tonight? We could both be very important people and see some badass crystals.

"There it is," Maggie says, hovering over my shoulder to read my texts. She sucks in a breath. "Honey!" Her voice is hushed and accusing. "You like him!"

"No, I don't."

"You're turning redder than my lipstick and girl it is *not* a sunburn."

I close my eyes. When I open them again, I know the truth is written all over my face. Maggie's lips form a little circle, then dip into a puppy frown. "Oh my gosh. Honey, that is so sweet. He seems great."

I shrug. "I don't know. Things are...weird between us. If he liked me, he could have said something by now."

"He's asking you on a date. What more do you need?"

I look at the text again.

"Is this a date? Or is it just a hang out?" I stare at my phone as if the answer will appear on the screen. It's a smart phone and all, but it's not that smart.

She makes a face. "What's your gut feeling?"

"My gut doesn't know what it wants."

Maggie pokes me in the stomach. "Make some decisions,

gut. Honey's happiness depends on it."

She's just joking, but I decide another slice of pizza might help my gut make up its mind. "Mason is different from the other guys," I say with my mouth full. "He's someone I might actually like…with the other guys, it was easy to go on just one date and then never talk to them again."

"Except for Furniture Guy," Maggie says.

I blow out a breath. The sting of Josh never texting me after our ice cream date still sucks when I think about it. I just try not to think about it. "It's still different with Mason. What if I like him? What if I *like*, like him?"

Maggie tosses her head back in a dramatic eye roll. "Liking someone is a good thing. If Luca isn't your soulmate, someone else might be. Sometimes you have to *like* like someone to know you're making the right decisions."

"You're phrasing that like it's advice, but it is not helpful."

Maggie laughs. "Here's something helpful: You should go with Mason to the museum thing."

"I don't know." I look up at the sky and take a deep breath.

"If you and Luca were still dating and happy, would you want to go to the museum for that gemstone thing?"

"Yes," I say without hesitation. "An exclusive viewing at the museum is the kind of thing you can't pass up."

Maggie rolls her hands in the air. "So go, you big dummy!"

I smirk, giddy at the idea of hanging out with Mason again. Even if it's not a date, it doesn't even have to be romantic. We can just be friends. Friends can go to museums together.

"Fine. I'll go because I want to see the exhibit. Not because I like him." I give Maggie a warning look. "You cannot make a big deal about this."

She nods quickly. "I won't. I promise."

Despite that promise, she's still pressed up against me to

watch me type out a reply. A few minutes later, Mason and I have made plans for him to pick me up at 5:30. I am so eager I can barely keep my stupid cheesy grin at bay, and the worst part is I have no idea if this is Date Number Four, or if it's just two friends hanging out.

CHAPTER TWENTY-TWO

Mason drives an old Chevy truck that smells like clean car smell and the polished dashboard shines like it's new. He talks enough for both of us on the drive to the Lonestar Museum of Natural Science. As it turns out, when he's not arrogantly correcting my knowledge of dinosaurs, or disagreeing with me in STEM Club, his voice is kind of cute. He should give up science and become a famous podcaster or read romance novel audiobooks for a living. I bet he could make a lot of money with that voice.

I learn that Mason's mom has worked at the Apple Valley grocery store for twenty years and his dad is a cook at an upscale restaurant. His twin little sisters are really into dance and are hoping to start going to competitions soon.

You can tell Mason is proud about going to college next year. Every time he mentions it he gets his child-like happiness in his eyes. He's eager to leave behind this small town and go find his place in the world. He comes from a family who is elated to see him succeed and will be happy to send him off to college. It must be nice to have your plans validated and supported instead of the guilt trip that's going on at my house. It's just after six o'clock, which means there are only six hours left of Decision Day. It's kind of a miracle that Luca hasn't bugged me about it yet. I know I will get home from this date and officially deny my acceptance to FLU, but until then, it's fun to entertain ideas of clicking the accept button instead.

The science museum is a sleek glass building that's narrow and several stories tall, nestled in the very center of the museum district. I've only been here on school field trips and occasionally during the summer with Luca and the moms. Back then the place was packed with students and parents, making the whole experience more of a lesson in patience than anything insightful or fun.

As Mason and I walk into the building, a single employee wearing a black suit stands in the lobby. He's a tall white man with a sharp jawline but kind eyes.

"Mason Ramos?" he asks.

Mason holds out the two VIP tickets that had been in his cupholder on the drive up here. "That's me."

I elbow Mason's arm. "How does the museum know your name?"

"Because I'm hella worldly and sophisticated."

I give him a look that says I'm not buying one word of that.

Mason grins, his shoulders falling in defeat. "This is my history teacher's husband."

"Jim Andrews," the man says. "Nice to meet you both. Mickey has told me a lot about you, Mason. Particularly your penchant for pointing out all of the mistakes in the textbook."

"What can I say?" Mason winks at me. "I'm a sucker for

factual information. Wait a minute – is Mr. Andrews' first name *Mickey*?"

"It's Michael," Jim says, his chiseled cheeks turning pink. "Mickey is a nickname, but don't let him know I accidentally told you that. He'd kill me."

Mason holds up his hands in innocence. "My lips are sealed, sir. But… WOW."

Jim's lip quirks. "You are exactly how he described you."

Mason grins. "A compliment, I'm sure."

"I feel bad for all of your teachers," I say. "And your parents… and friends…"

"Oh, she's got jokes." Mason wraps an arm around my shoulders and squeezes me close to him. It's a quick gesture, over before I can even register it, but it fills my entire body with a glorious warm feeling, and as soon as he lets go, I'm aching to touch him again.

"Ready for your VIP exhibit?" Jim says, leading us to a velvet rope partition that separates the lobby from an entryway. "We aren't expecting anyone else tonight, so you'll have the entire showroom to yourselves. It closes at nine." He unhooks one end of the velvet rope and pulls it back. "Enjoy your trip through the crystals of India."

The room is dark and cool, illuminated only by single spotlights that flood over each beautiful piece of crystal. The shining jewels are all kept safe in customized clear boxes, which is a real shame because the sparkling pretties are practically begging me to touch them.

Mason is silent as we explore the exhibit. There's a special reverence in the room, thanks to the stunning geologic formations that only Mother Nature herself could make.

"These crystals were formed in beds of basalt rock more than 65 million years ago. They were created by colossal lava flows from volcanic eruptions," Mason reads from the placard in front of us. "Paleontologists speculate that these volcanic eruptions could have contributed to the extinction of the dinosaurs."

"Whoa."

Mason nods at my incredibly articulate observation. "Crazy how something so beautiful can come from something so destructive."

I look over at him. I know my mouth is hanging open like one of the Neanderthal statues we passed in the museum lobby, but I can't help it. Mason's words just hit me somewhere deep, somewhere raw.

Something so beautiful can come from something so destructive.

Destruction. That's what would happen if I split with Luca for good. Total, utter, chaotic destruction. My relationship would fall apart, making my lifelong best friend my ex. My life would rip in half, and I'd lose my second parents and Rudo and all of Luca's cousins and grandparents who have become my own family over the years.

Could something beautiful rise from the ashes of that kind of destruction? Or would it all be for nothing? What if I ripped apart my entire world and found nothing but wasteland?

"Hey," Mason says softly, pulling me from my thoughts.

I look over at him and he smiles, a soft, vulnerable look I've never seen on him. "Thanks for coming with me tonight."

"Thanks for inviting me," I say, shoving my hands in my back pockets. "Let me guess, everyone else in STEM Club was busy and couldn't go?"

"I only asked you." He walks to the next gemstone.

I walk up next to him, looking at his reflection in the shiny glass case in front of us. "Why?"

I want him to say it. I don't even know why. It's not like I'm going to college with him in the fall. After graduation, I'll probably never see him again.

"I like you," he says, turning toward me. "I think I always have."

Everything goes very still. Suddenly every single STEM Club meeting flashes through my mind, but in a different way. I imagine if Mason had told me this years ago, if instead of petty arguments, we were flirting and holding hands in that empty science lab. I think of how my life would have been if Luca was just a neighbor and close friend and not my boyfriend. If I had dated Mason instead.

"Why didn't you tell me sooner?" My voice shatters the awkward silence. "Like, the second Luca and I broke up?"

"I didn't want to be one of five dates."

Fair enough. I put my palms over the sides of my head and take a breath. "It's only the oldest plotline in every story ever," I mumble, smiling to myself at the thought of Vu's words.

"What?"

"Nothing." I walk toward the next glass-enclosed gemstone because my body needs to move or all this contemplation might make my muscles explode. "My nickname for you is my mortal enemy."

"That's a little harsh," Mason says. "We're not *mortal* enemies. I'm always on your side when Anna brings up Star Wars."

"Okay, but you argue with me on every other thing."

He shakes his head. "That's an exaggeration."

"See? You're arguing with me over this sentence!"

"Not that sentence, technically, but the one before it."

I glare at him until we both laugh.

"I'm sorry," he says softly. "I don't want to be mortal

enemies. It's just that when we're bickering, it's easier to remind myself that you'll never be mine."

I draw in a sharp breath. I'm not used to this kind of honesty.

"Never is a long time," I breathe.

Mason's fingers brush against mine, sending a shocking feeling straight to my core. When he touches me, he's like electricity and the grounding wire are fighting for control. All of my senses light up when we're close. It takes much longer than it should for me to realize what's happening. This is the fireworks Maggie talks about. I feel them bursting in every cell of my body. Tiny little life-changing fireworks.

His hand lingers there, his fingers pressed lightly against mine. I flex my fingers, letting them hook into his. When I look into his eyes, he is somehow closer than I thought, his silky dark hair shining under the spotlight, a few strands of it swooping just over his brow.

He squeezes my hand. "You're not going to Fault Line, are you?"

"I don't think so." My voice sounds a million miles away. I shake my head softly, every single thing I regret about myself floating around in my mind. I can't focus on anything but that cute quirk of his lips. The way his brows pull together when I'm talking and I know he's actually, truly listening to me.

"There's still time to change your mind." With our hands still intertwined, he moves onto the next crystal, an opalescent flowering rock that's the size of a baseball. I follow, not wanting to let go.

"Mason." The word is a whisper. A question, and an answer. Hopeless, and hopeful.

My heart is in my throat. My pulse is in my ears. All the parts of me are all jumbled up, tossed in a rock tumbler and spun until the rough edges are gone and all that remains is a brand new Honey Blackwell. One who knows what she wants and takes it. With only a few hours left to decide my future, I've just made another decision.

His hand cups my cheek, his fingers warm and soft and filled with all of the kindness I see reflected in his eyes. He smells like the ocean, and boy, and something citrusy, something distinctly Mason. His eyes are dark, two obsidian gemstones glistening under the soft museum lighting. His thumb slides down my cheek. "Would you turn and run if I kissed you?"

"Where would I run to?" I ask with a sly grin. "You're my ride home."

"Fair point," Mason says. I feel his other arm tighten around my waist. With my hand on his chest, I can feel his heartbeat, pounding away as if it's running a marathon. His forehead presses to mine. "I'm going to kiss you now," he breathes.

I close my eyes, my grin wider than the great state of Texas. "Please do."

CHAPTER TWENTY-THREE

Mason's lips are soft and sweet. I don't know how long we stand here, surrounded by the glittering majestic crystals, our bodies pressed close and our lips closer. Probably a couple of minutes.

It feels like no time at all.

Mason stands eye level with me. When we break apart, I'm looking right into his eyes. My hands are on his chest, but I want to wrap them around his neck instead. I want to know if his hair feels as soft as it looks. I want so much more than what we have in this very moment because I'm worried it'll all go away.

"Ahem."

We jump, stepping apart. The polite throat-clearing came from Jim, who stands several feet away at the opening of the exhibit. "The museum is officially closed."

"Thank you," Mason says, nodding. "We'll be on our way."

He reaches for my hand and I give it to him. We don't say anything on the walk out of the museum and back to his truck, but the electricity between us is louder than a freight train. I don't think I'm the only one who can hear it, either.

My teeth dig into my bottom lip for the entire drive home. *I kissed Mason.* Mason – who is cute and irritating and an insufferable know-it-all. Mason who I am now crushing on so hard.

I. Kissed. Mason.

That whole "butterflies in your stomach" phrase isn't accurate at all. That's not what this feels like. It's a visceral, tugging and twisting of my insides, not in my stomach but right beneath my ribcage. A fluttering that feels like a giant is squeezing my heart and making it jump all over the place. Butterflies are light, dainty, and easily squishable.

This feeling is something else entirely. It's almost painful, but I like it at the same time. I also hate it, but I don't ever want it to go away. Kissing Mason has awakened a million new possibilities for me. If I can kiss Mason, I can do anything. I *could* go to Fault Line University. I could go right up to my room, log into the website, and click accept. I could totally do it.

Everything else would just have to fall into place.

When Mason pulls into my driveway, something feels off, but I guess I'm just filled with nervous energy over what I'm about to do. I smile over my nerves. "Thank you for tonight."

"Thank *you* for tonight," he says back.

"Hey, come up with your own sentences!" I say, playfully smacking his arm.

He grins. We stare at each other for one ridiculously flirtatious second. Then I summon up the sense to tell him goodbye. As Mason backs out of my driveway, I realize why everything feels weird. It's not just the date—my house looks different. My parents' cars are gone and all the lights are off, even though it's almost eleven at night. Luca's house is also dark. Only Jill's car is in the driveway. Not even a porch light is on...and their porch light is *always* on.

Standing on my porch, I dig in my purse to find my phone. Seventeen missed calls make all the blood drain from my face. Mom usually calls once and then texts me if I don't answer. Seventeen calls can't be good.

"Honey!" she shouts as a way of answering my call. "Where are you? Why didn't you answer?"

"I was out with a friend and my phone was on silent. What's going on?"

"Sweetheart, Luca was in a car wreck. He's okay—" she says quickly when I gasp. "He's stable. He's going to be fine. We're all here at Stonebrook Memorial. He's asking for you."

"Can you come get me?"

"Take Jill's car. She said the keys are on the kitchen counter."

My heart pounds on the short drive to the hospital. Mom meets me at the large automatic glass doors. She's wearing leggings and a baggy shirt which means she must have rushed over here the second she heard about Luca. I always thought it would take an apocalypse to make my mom leave the house in leggings.

"Third floor," she says, wrapping an arm around me.

I'm shaking as I let her guide me through the busy corridors. I've never been in a hospital before. The sterile smell burns my nose. Nurses powerwalk up and down the hallways, sometimes pushing a cart or gurney. The intercom disperses coded information that's spoken way too quickly for me to understand. This place is well balanced chaos. If only my mind could behave the same way.

Mom pushes open a heavy door that has Luca's name scribbled on a small whiteboard next to it. Our parents crowd the small room. The dads are standing very close together, talking in hushed tones. Jill sits in a chair next to Luca's bed.

Oh no, Luca.

My first instinct is to run up to him but fear holds me back. Luca lays surrounded by wires and tubes and heaps of white blankets. The left side of his head has been shaved down to the scalp, where a blood-red jagged line has been stapled shut. His face is splotched with purple and blue and his left arm is in a cast.

Despite it all, he smiles when he sees me. "It's not as bad as it looks."

"What happened?"

"Ice cream happened." If his lip wasn't split open, he'd be smirking.

I lift an eyebrow.

Jill stands up and offers me her chair. "Come sit down. We need to head home and get ready for work tomorrow." She squeezes my arm and then she and the rest of the parents just walk right out of here as if Luca isn't looking like a zombie right now.

I watch the door click closed behind them. "I can't believe they just left."

"I told them to," he says, reaching out a hand toward me. "They've been here for hours and I was ready for them to leave, but they wouldn't until you got here."

As I reach out and take his hand, these last few hours of swoony, happy, gushy, feelings get sucked into the massive black void that is real life. I was kissing a boy while Luca was getting his head cracked open. This is not okay.

I look into the eye that isn't halfway swollen shut. "Please tell me how ice cream did this to you?"

"I was eating a chocolate dipped ice cream cone while

driving." He breathes in, wincing a bit. "It slipped out of my hand and rolled under the gas pedal. I went right in that ditch off Everett Street. Pretty sure my truck is totaled."

"I can't believe ice cream would betray you like that," I say, squeezing his fingers. The big scary IV taped to the top of his hand makes me not want to touch it, so I hold his fingers instead.

"I have a concussion, broken arm, and lots and lots of contusions and lacerations," he says, dragging in another breath. Talking seems painful for him. His head falls back onto the pillow. "That's the fancy doctor talk for being totally wrecked."

"How much pain are you in?" I point a finger at him. "And don't lie to me because I'll know."

His one good eye blinks. "A lot."

I don't know when I started crying, but now I'm wiping off tears with the back of my hand. Seeing him like this breaks me apart at the seams. The worst part is my lips still tingle from the memory of Mason. No, the *worst* part is that I'm even still thinking about Mason.

"Can you stay with me?" Luca asks, his fingers lacing between mine. "They're keeping me overnight for observation on my head."

"Of course I'll stay."

That one eye looks relieved. The other is shiny and red. It hurts me to look at him like this.

"Do you want to go home and get a pillow and blanket or something?"

"No," I say, dragging the only chair in the room right up to the side of his hospital bed. "I'm not leaving you. You get some sleep. I'll be right here."

"You da best."

I look over the machines on the wall. He has an IV bag, a beepy thing that shows his pulse which is currently 122, and a blood pressure cuff on his arm that's hooked up to another machine. I know it could be worse, but it's still bad. A stupid ice cream cone could have killed him. The worst part is knowing that if we never broke up, he wouldn't be here. I know it with a certainty because every time we get ice cream I sit in the middle seat and hold his cone for him. He'll stick his tongue out and I swirl the cone around for him. It's just one of those things we do, and today he had to do it without me.

My guilt morphs into something more than just a feeling. There's a real, actual blackened tumor-like ball of guilt in my stomach right now. It's probably some gross medical phenomenon that reality TV show doctors would love to get their hands on. *The first ever tangible evidence of guilt.*

Luca falls quickly asleep, leaving me to assess the situation. All I have on me is my phone, which is at 25% battery, and the clothes on my back. A table across the small room has two pillows on it and I grab them, shoving them into the crack between my chair and Luca's bed. Then I pull my feet up to my chest and try to get comfortable in a chair that seems to have been designed to be as uncomfortable as possible.

"Honey?" Luca's voice is so soft I almost don't hear it over the hum of the machines. His hand feels around until he finds mine. "I love you," he whispers.

"I love you, too."

We don't have to be dating for me to love him. I love him like I love my family. I don't know what I would do if I lost him.

I sit here, my head leaning on a squished up pillow, while I watch him sleep. I keep an eye on the machines, and the pulse one finally goes down to 80, which seems like more than it should be but better than 122. Luca is an athlete. He used to brag about his resting heart rate of 55.

A nurse with curly auburn hair walks in wearing Texas A&M scrubs. The sight of that logo messes with my head.

"Hi," she whispers to me as she checks his chart. "I'm Melanie, the night nurse. Will you be staying here overnight?"

"Am I allowed to?" I ask.

"You family?"

"Yes."

"Then go for it," she says, moving over to Luca's IV bag, which she changes out for a new one. "There's a lever on the back of that chair that folds it down into a bed."

"Really? You're a lifesaver."

She chuckles. "I'll bring you an extra blanket. And here's the button you can press if he wakes up and needs anything."

After she finishes checking on Luca, who sleeps through the whole thing, I lay down in the chair-bed and count the staples in Luca's skull. Fourteen. No one in our families have ever been hurt this bad. I don't know how to handle it, or what's to come in the weeks that follow. All I know is I can't leave Luca at a time when he needs me. Hopefully he's healed before college starts in the fall.

Oh shit. College!

I bolt out of the chair and dig my phone out of my purse. I would need to log in and accept Fault Line before midnight— but I'm not even sure I want to now. My phone screen blinks awake, showing a picture of Luca's dog Rudo. It's still weird getting used to my phone's wallpaper not being a photo of Luca and me, but I changed it shortly after we broke up. On the phone, right above Rudo's furry head, is the second worst thing that's happened today.

It's 1:18 in the morning. I've missed the Decision Day

deadline. In a panic, I go to my email and click the link and try to sign in anyway. Maybe their website is set to a different time zone. Maybe there's still time.

I get an error message. *This request has expired.*

A single tear falls down my cheek. I look up at Luca, who sleeps soundly. I see Nurse Melanie walk briskly past the open crack in the doorway, her maroon scrubs seeming to mock me with their little logos. I guess I always knew I wouldn't be going to Fault Line University. But now it's official. I waited too long and the choice was made for me. I went on a date and Luca almost died. And despite it all, I can't stop picturing Mason's grin from underneath the museum lights. More tears roll down my cheeks.

I don't even know which heartache is making me cry.

CHAPTER TWENTY-FOUR

"Knock, knock."

I blink awake. Everything about waking up in a hospital is weird—I would know because I woke up a dozen times last night to the various sounds in here—but that voice sounded a lot like my best friend.

"Psst. Honey!"

I turn to the door. It *is* my best friend. Maggie stands just outside the room, smiling nervously at me through the two-inch crack in the open door. I don't know why the nurses never fully close it after their million trips in here to check on Luca.

I wave for her to come inside while I try to stand up. It'll take a minute to work out the muscle cramps in my neck from sleeping on this chair. Even when it's reclined, it still sucks. And it smells like a daycare. Must be the Lysol.

"How's he doing?" she whispers, wincing at Luca's sleeping form.

"He'll be okay," I whisper back. "They're worried about his

concussion and his heart rate was really high all night, but it got lower after I got here."

"Aww," Maggie says, putting a hand to her mouth.

I don't think my presence is what lowered his high heart rate. At least... I don't think so.

Maggie digs in her purse. "I brought you a charger," she whispers, holding out a portable battery pack with a charge cord.

"You're the best." I plug my phone in, rescuing it from its four percent battery life.

Maggie walks to the other side of Luca's bed, her eyes roaming over the machines and his injuries. "Wow," she says softly. "You look like shit."

Luca chuckles. I didn't realize he was awake and I jump up and grab his fingers. He slowly rolls his head over to look at me. The swelling in his left eye has gone down significantly and he looks almost like himself if you ignore the half-mohawk, gnarly stiches, and all those bruises and small cuts.

"How are you?" I say, trying to smooth out all the worry from my face.

"Oh I'm great." He smirks just like old times. "I ran a 5k before you woke up."

I roll my eyes.

"I think he'll make a full recovery," Maggie says, playfully smacking his knee on top of the blankets. "By the way Luca, you're a social media star right now. Or, should I say, your truck is the social media star." She holds up her phone.

Someone snapped a photo of Luca's truck—the remains of it at least—loaded onto a flatbed trailer on the side of the road. Everyone knows it's his truck because of the big R&B logo on the back window, which is somehow the only window that didn't shatter.

I take the phone from her and zoom in on the photo. You can barely tell it used to be a truck. One of the guys from the track team posted the photo and there's already a hundred comments and it's only eight in the morning. I give the phone back to Maggie. "You're lucky to be alive."

The serious conversation is cut short when my stomach lets out a loud, rumbly growl. The last time I ate was during lunch yesterday. I had been too nervous to eat something for dinner before meeting up with Mason. Hard to believe that museum date was just a few hours ago.

"Let's go get some breakfast," Maggie says. "I saw the breakfast cart down the hallway so they'll bring Luca's food in here soon."

"I can't leave him," I say.

"You can go." He squeezes my hand. "I gotta ask a nurse to help me take a leak anyway. It'll be less embarrassing if you're not here, so take your time."

Maggie and I make our way down to the cafeteria. This place is a huge, complicated maze, but if you follow the signs on the wall, navigating it isn't too bad. I get a chocolate chip muffin that's twice the size of my fist and a large coffee. Maggie gets the same muffin and an iced cinnamon latte which comes from a vending machine of questionable cleanliness.

"I feel like it's the wrong time to say this but..." Maggie peels off the wrapper from her muffin then looks at me through her long eyelashes. "What happened on your date?"

I shake my head. "Doesn't matter. Nothing matters."

"Does that mean it didn't go well?"

"It doesn't matter what happened with Mason. Because I'm staying here in Stonebrook."

She sets the muffin down and laces her fingers together on top of the table. "Explain."

"The date was amazing, okay? I even kissed him. It was the best. But then I got home and rushed here to be with Luca and his heart rate didn't get lower until I got here for him. He needs me, Maggie. And I was so caught up in everything that I forgot to accept Fault Line until it was too late."

I'm trembling as I shake my head, trying to hold it together. "I missed out on my college. And the worst part is, I guess I always knew I wasn't going to Colorado. My place is here, with Luca, and R&B Construction. This is where I belong."

"So you're getting back with Luca," she says.

I nod. "This is my life. It's where I belong."

"If you're happy, I'm happy," Maggie says, reaching out and putting her hand on top of mine for a moment. "Are you happy?"

"I am." Or at least I will be. My stomach is churning with a dozen emotions, but when the dust settles and Luca's bones heal, everything will go back to normal. We can get back together and graduate and go to A&M together. Just as planned.

After a sugar and caffeine breakfast, we go to the hospital's gift shop on the first floor. I pick out several Get Well Soon balloons, a stuffed bear with a broken arm, and one of every sports magazine they have. Buying him all these gifts won't take away the kiss I shared with Mason, but at least it helps assuage some of my guilt.

Luca deserves so much better than the girlfriend I've been. He's always been there for me, and yet I wanted to leave him and our family and everything just for some fancy college that's no better than A&M. I won't make this mistake again.

Maggie helps me carry all of the stuff I bought back up to the third floor. We somehow take the wrong elevator and end up at the opposite end of the hallway from Luca's room. While we walk back, a girl about our age with shoulder-length dark hair and a white sundress reads the name on the sign next to Luca's door. Then she walks right on in. I look to Maggie. "Who the hell is that?"

She shrugs.

I pick up the pace and stop just outside the doorway. Like Maggie had done a couple hours ago, I peek into the open space where the door never closes.

"Oh my god!" the girl says, rushing up to Luca. "Baby, you look terrible."

Baby?

"I'm better now," Luca says. I can't see him behind the girl's gorgeous beach wave hair, but it sounds like he's smiling.

She puts her hands on each side of his face and then kisses him right on the lips.

Just like that. This strange new girl kisses my boyfriend.

The shopping bags of gifts suddenly weigh a hundred pounds. I set them on the floor outside of the door, then I take the weighted bundle of balloon ribbons from Maggie's hand and drop them as well. I open my mouth to say something to her, but nothing comes out. All I can do is turn and walk away.

I can't unsee what just happened. I can't walk backward and rewind time and go back and fix my life before it got all screwed up. Before, there was a small crack in my relationship, a slight little chip that bothered me like a blister, a scratch. I could have fixed the crack, healed the blister. I could have made it all better. But I didn't.

I took a sledgehammer and shattered the crack to pieces by suggesting that Luca and I break up and date other people. Like a geode that's been cracked open and put on display, I can't ever put us back together again. Luca has moved on without me.

CHAPTER TWENTY-FIVE

Our dining room is a mess, which can only mean one thing: the moms are planning a graduation party. With Luca's night in the hospital, losing my dream college, and that beautiful girl in the white dress, the annual event completely slipped my mind this year. When I walk downstairs on Saturday morning and see the flurry of papers, folders, fabric samples, and the moms' laptops open on the dining table, I remember exactly what time it is.

R&B Construction owns the only building in the town that's big enough to host an event of this size, and every year for the past decade, the moms have hosted Stonebrook High's Project Graduation there, free of charge. They say it's their way of giving back to the community, but everyone who is close to the moms know they just love planning parties and will find any excuse to do so.

It's been a few days since the accident. Luca got to go home yesterday. He doesn't know I saw that girl kiss him. He also doesn't know I've exhausted all social media snooping methods and still have no clue who she is. The weird thing is that he's been acting so normal. He texted me goodnight last night for the first time since we broke up.

I pull my hair into a twisted bun and put on a smile as I walk past the moms. "Morning."

"Good, you're up," Mom says. She's still wearing the gray sweatpants she wore to bed last night, but she's traded her faded, oversized Astro's sleep shirt for a black tank top. Her hair is the same shade of dark brown as my roots, but it's frizzier, piled on top of her head in a bun.

She hands me a list of store names and addresses. "We need your help collecting the silent auction items today."

"We have three times the donations this year," Jill says proudly. "All because we made a Facebook post asking for donations instead of calling around like we used to do."

Jill is more put together than my mom, wearing jeans and a blue button up blouse that has little white arrows all over it. Her signature cat-eye eyeliner is perfectly in place and she smiles up at me while she sips from her coffee mug. "Social media is amazing."

"It's good timing too, because all the money we'll raise this year will go toward making the best graduation party ever," Mom says, her attention on her laptop. "It'll be the greatest Project Grad we've ever done. Only the best for Honey and Luca."

Jill sucks in an excited breath through her teeth as she grins at me. "I can't believe our babies are graduating this year! Time flies."

"It really does," Mom says. "I am so proud of you and Luca. You're both great kids and you're turning into amazing people."

"Amen to that," Jill says, holding up her coffee mug. Mom lifts her own mug and they do a toast. "To us," Jill says.

"To us?" Mom questions, her brows pulling together.

Jill shrugs. "We're the ones who created and raised two beautiful children. I say we deserve all the credit."

Mom laughs and they clink their mugs together. "To us."

I go to my room to throw on some clothes. My phone beeps.

Mason (like the jar): I heard about Luca's
    wreck. Is he okay?

People have been reaching out to me nonstop since that photo of Luca's mangled truck went Stonebrook Viral. I'm used to answering questions about it, but talking to Mason is more than weird. We haven't spoken since he dropped me off at home several nights ago.

Me: Yes, he'll be okay.

Mason (like the jar): That's good. Let me know
    if you need anything.

I don't even know what to say to that. Luca has a new girl, so I shouldn't feel guilty about Mason anymore. But Mason is going to FLU in the fall. I'm not.

My lungs can't seem to take in a full breath until I'm out of the house and in Mom's car. I point the air conditioning vent at my face and breathe in deeply just to remind myself that I can. I'm not suffocating, my life just feels like I am. I toss my phone into the cupholder and back out of the driveway.

Mom arranged the list in order of closest businesses to the ones farther away, so I prop the paper up on the dashboard and start checking them off one by one. Most places donate gift cards, which are small and simple to stash in the console.

The Dog Shack donated a gift basket filled with dog toys and treats, and it takes up half the backseat. The Hobby Hole donated a similar gift basket filled with craft supplies, and I find room for it in the trunk, stuffed between a toolbox donated from the hardware store and a cake decorating kit from my favorite bakery.

I check my list, folding the paper back after each location has been visited. I have two stops left, both of them in Apple Valley. After getting a gift certificate for a year's worth of car washes, I drive to the grocery store that's last on my list.

Apple Valley Foods is a small building for a grocery store, but it's packed to the brim with everything you could need. I don't know how they do it. I make my way inside and head toward the customer service desk. The woman behind the counter looks old enough to be someone's great-grandmother. Her nametag says Dottie, and it's engraved with *50 years of service* underneath her name.

"Oh yes," she says, nodding at me after I tell her why I'm here. She points a knobby finger toward the cash registers. "Go ask the woman at the first register. She knows how to activate the gift cards and she's expecting you."

I smile and thank her, then make my way over to the register. This woman is short, with dark hair that's pulled into a tight ponytail and bright pink lipstick that makes her smile look youthful.

"How can I help you?" she says. Her nametag says Nicole and *20 years of service.*

"I'm picking up a donation for the Stonebrook High Project Graduation silent auction."

"That's a mouthful," she says with a laugh.

"Tell me about it. I've had to say that like twenty times today."

She chuckles and then retrieves an envelope with the store's logo embossed on the front and activates a gift card.

"Honey?"

I know it's Mason the moment he says my name, but seeing him standing here in front of me feels like a surprise so unexpected I can hardly keep my balance.

"Hi," I say, my voice sharper and weirder than usual.

"Is this *the* Honey?" the woman at the register asks him.

He smirks. "How many Honeys do you know, Mom? Because I only know the one."

Mom?

She puts the gift card in the fancy envelope and then holds it out to me. "It's so nice to meet you," she says, giving me a knowing sort of smile that only a mother can make. It's the same smile the moms give me when they talk about my future marriage to Luca. "Mason has told me all about you."

"Has he?" I give Mason a look, and to my surprise, the usually cocky expression on his face has turned to one of total chagrin.

"I told her *about* you," he says, putting emphasis on that word. "Not *all* about you. I don't even know all about you." With that, he gives his mother a glare—a polite glare, but a glare nonetheless.

"Congratulations on your college acceptance," she says warmly. "I bet your parents are so proud."

"Yeah." I bite out the lie as convincingly as possible. Clearly Mason didn't tell her everything. "Thank you."

A customer appears behind us and starts unloading their cart on the conveyer belt. Thank you, Grocery Gods, for giving me this excuse to leave. "I should get going," I say, stepping out of the way.

"You should come to dinner," Mason's mom says while she

starts scanning the customer's items. "We'll make pancit. Are you free tonight?"

"You don't have to," Mason says quickly.

"What do you say?" his mom asks while ringing up the customer. Thanks to the loud beeping of the barcode scanner, I don't think she heard what he told me.

"I'll be there," I say with a smile that mirrors her own.

"Wonderful!" She puts a bag of apples on the scale and punches in the produce code without even looking at the keypad. I guess when you've worked somewhere for two decades, you know that kind of thing by heart.

"I'll walk you out," Mason says, falling into step with me.

We stop in front of my mom's car and a familiar feeling settles into the air around us. It's thick and murky and full of regret. It's the feeling of my heart that wants to be around Mason at all costs, in a war with my brain that knows better than to make this into something it's not.

"So... dinner at my house," Mason says, shoving his hands in his pockets. "I feel like I should apologize now for my parents. They'll be so friendly and welcoming that you'll want to run away screaming. And my sisters..." He heaves a sigh. "Thirteen-year-old girls are the worst. All they do is make fun of me."

"Sounds like my kind of party," I say. "Maybe I could give your sisters some pointers."

He rolls his eyes. "You're my friend. You should be on *my* side!"

"I'll try my best," I say, opening the car door. "But making fun of you is just *so* much fun."

"Well, I can't let you miss out on making fun of me." He bites back a grin. "I'll text you my address."

CHAPTER TWENTY-SIX

I park Mom's car on the curb, right in front of the painted numbers that match Mason's address. His home is in an older part of town, where every house on the street looks like someone's grandma lives in it. The ranch style home is blue, with faded white shutters, and two older cars in the driveway. Mason's truck is parked on the side of the road. I send him a text to let him know I'm here and then I walk up to the door. The air gets thicker as I approach, or maybe that's just me—all nervous energy and self-conscious worries making my throat close up.

This is exactly the kind of thing that other people experience. High school students, college students. Anyone going on a first date for the first time has to deal with this. The dreaded walk up to the front door where you'll knock and probably have to talk to a parent. It's terrifying. I don't know how other people do it once, much less the five or more times it takes for them to find their soulmate.

I never had to meet Luca's parents. I've known them since the day I was born.

My home ec teacher is all about new experiences. She's always saying we should step out of our comfort zone as much as we can. That we should try new things and be scared and do it anyway—that it all makes us more well-rounded humans in the end.

Meeting Mason's family totally counts as one of those experiences. But staying with Luca and never dating anyone else seems so much easier.

The front door swings open before I knock, and Mason is standing there. Thank God for text messages. Otherwise who knows who would have answered the door.

He pushes open the screen door and greets me with that adorable side grin of his. "Hi."

"Hi."

"We almost got lucky," Mason says as he lets me inside. "My sisters were *this close* to going to a friend's house tonight. But then that fell through, so now we're stuck with them."

I chuckle. "I'm sure they're not that bad."

"Spoken like someone who clearly doesn't have thirteen-year-old twin sisters."

Mason's living room is empty, but the mouth-watering smell of food and the sounds of music and talking tell me that everyone is in the kitchen. Having already met his mom today, I'm sure this will be fine, but I'm still so nervous I can barely walk. How do regular people do this kind of thing? Why would anyone date five different people and have to meet five different parents? It's one thing to step out of your comfort zone every now and then but right now I feel like I've launched myself off a cliff of discomfort. And if my home ec teacher is right about these types of experiences making us more well-rounded, I'll have no sharp edges when this is all over.

"Our dinner guest is here," Mason says as he leads me into the kitchen. "Please don't embarrass me."

I think that last part is a statement to his whole family, but his sisters look the most offended.

"We're nice people!" one of them says before waving at me and turning back to her phone. Both girls are absorbed with their phones while sitting next to each other at a bar-height kitchen table. The family resemblance is strong. They all have the same incredibly dark eyes, soft features, and silky black hair.

"We're totally nice," the other twin says, flashing me a devious smile.

Mason's expression tells me he doesn't believe that for one second. "Iris and Ivy," he says, motioning to the identical girls. Ivy happens to be wearing a green shirt, which is kind of the color of an ivy plant, so this is how I decide to tell them apart tonight. If I call identical twins by their names, that's sure to win me some brownie points with the Ramos family. Mason gestures to me. "This is my friend, Honey."

"Hi, Mason's-new-*friend*," Iris says, batting her eyelashes at me. Her sister giggles.

"Okay, that's enough of them." Mason takes my arm and leads me into the kitchen where his parents are preparing a meal that smells better than anything I've ever smelled in my own kitchen.

Mason's mom gives me a quick one-armed hug. "Nice to see you again, Honey."

She's wearing a dark blue apron with white ruffles on the bottom. The ruffles are made from Houston Texan's fabric which has the football team's logo all over it.

"So nice to meet you," Mason's dad says. He waves at me with his spatula while he stands in front of the stove. He's wearing a matching apron, dark blue with the logo fabric as a large pocket on the front instead of as ruffles along the edges. "Hope you like bihon pancit!"

"I'm... not sure what that is," I say honesty. "But it smells great."

"It's Filipino fried rice noodles," Mason says, reaching over and popping a grilled shrimp in his mouth. "Dad's specialty. When he was trying to win over my mom, he learned the most basic dish from the Philippines and cooked it for her."

Mrs. Ramos smacks her son's hand away. "No stealing bites before dinner."

"Sorry, Ma." Mason gives me a sheepish smile. "Want something to drink? We have literally every soda and store-bought drink possible."

"The perks of working at a grocery store," Mrs. Ramos tells me. "Employee discount."

There's a large Fault Line University pennant sticker across the refrigerator door. I stare at it while Mason reaches inside and gets two sodas for us. I might have the same pennant had I accepted my dream college. I guess it doesn't matter now.

Dinner is served up in colorful dishware and on crocheted trivets in the middle of the table. Most of their décor seems handmade, or thrifted. Aunt Bree would love it here. It's cozy and colorful and warm.

Mr. Ramos serves everyone a large bowl of the pancit bihon, which is made with soft rice noodles, vegetables, chicken, and shrimp with some kind of sauce mixed in. The flavor is amazing.

"What's the celebration?" I ask, noticing a silver foil banner hanging from the wall. It says CONGRATULATIONS.

"Nothing," Mason says. "My mom put it up months ago

when I got accepted into FLU and she hasn't taken it down yet."

"I'm not ready to stop celebrating!" Mrs. Ramos says. "College is a big deal."

"Scholarships are a big deal," his dad says, motioning with his fork. "It was never a surprise that he would get into college. I knew he'd get in. What I didn't know is how we'd pay for it."

"Sacrifices," Mrs. Ramos says. "All good things are worth making sacrifices."

"He'll be the first in our family to go to college," Mr. Ramos says with a pride in his voice that's very parental. "And then our girls will be the second and third."

"I bet your parents are thrilled too," Mrs. Ramos says, giving me a warm smile. "Getting into FLU is quite the accomplishment."

The food in my mouth suddenly loses all of its flavor. I nod slowly. "It was...unexpected."

"But so worth it," she says.

Of course she thinks I'm going to FLU in the fall. Mason thinks I'm going. I'll have to break the news to him sometime, but doing it in front of his family is not the right time.

"What do your parents do?" Mr. Ramos asks.

"My mom is a real estate agent. My dad remodels houses and flips them."

"That sounds rewarding," he says.

I nod. "They both love their job. I'm supposed to work at the family business one day—after college."

"That's where I know you!" Iris drops her fork with a clang and stares at me, then grabs her sister's arm. "She's Honey Blackwell!"

"Ooooh," Ivy says, nodding eagerly. "*That's* who she is."

"How do you know her?" Mason asks.

"She's the girl on the funny Facebook videos! R&B Construction –" Iris says, singing the words in a familiar tune.

Her sister joins in, singing the awful jingle the dads made up two summers ago. "If we can't do it, then it can't be done!"

"You've seen those videos?" I say. The dads love their mostly silly and slightly helpful home improvement videos. One video on how to install a TV over a fireplace went viral when Dad dropped and shattered the TV a couple years ago. It made them the talk of the town, and they loved the attention so they still make those silly videos on occasion.

The girls nod. "Your company is like, famous."

I chuckle and look down at my food. "I'll be sure to let my dad know he has fans."

Family dinners with Mason's family is a lot like dinners with my family, only I don't know all the inside jokes. His parents are nice, and his sisters are a bit nosy, but I have a good time. After we eat, Mason and I end up in the front yard where he shows me the rain gauge science project he made in sixth grade that's still functional.

Someone lets the family dog out of his kennel, and he runs right up to me begging for some attention. Chippy is a black chihuahua mix with a small bit of his left ear missing. I'm guessing that's how he got his name.

"You're so tiny!" I say, scooping the little dog into my arms. Rudo's head is the size of this entire dog.

"There they are!" one of his sisters calls out. Both girls appear on the front porch.

Ivy, with the green sweater, turns to me. "Hey, isn't your boyfriend that super hot guy from the videos?"

"Oh my gosh, yes he is so hot," Iris says, her jaw dropping open as she agrees with her sister. "Is he still your boyfriend?"

"Luca?" I say, shaking my head furiously as my whole body heats up. I am acutely aware of Mason going rigid next to me. "No. He's not my boyfriend. Not... not anymore."

"That's too bad," Iris says. "He's on a lot of the videos, too. Like that new video that talks about college." She holds out her phone, which is on the dad's YouTube video titled: *Our kids are going to Texas A&M!*

Ivy's smug look is impossible to miss. She folds her arms over her chest. "You said you were going to Colorado but this video says you're going to A&M. So which is it?"

"I got into both colleges," I say.

"But which one are you going to?"

"Ivy, *shut up*," Mason says. "Honey is a guest and y'all are being annoying, so go away."

They leave, but the damage is done.

Mason tugs on the leather bracelets around his wrist. "Are you really going to A&M?"

I look down at the tiny dog in my arms, and even Chippy doesn't seem to be happy anymore. I nod.

"So... I guess you're getting back together with Luca?"

Chippy squirms so I set him down. "What makes you think that?"

"Well..." he stumbles over his words before looking up at me. "I don't know why else you would stay here. I thought we both wanted out of this town."

The look in his eyes brings actual pain to my chest. Then it morphs into anger. I can't stand the way he's staring at me, like I'm some disappointing loser.

"I can choose to stay here on my own."

"You would never stay here on your own," he says, his voice clipped. Confused. "You're staying because of him."

"How dare you think I'm staying specifically because of

Luca. I don't make every decision based on a boy." Anger rises up, making me storm off the porch and to my car.

"Honey, don't go," Mason says, jogging after me.

"How dare you," I say again.

"I just wanted to know where I stand." Mason looks down at the cracks in the driveway. "Was I just one of your five dates, or was I something more?"

I swallow. If I tell him how I truly feel, we'll both be hurt in the long run when he goes to college and I stay here. Might as well get hurt now. "You were one date," I say, opening my car door. "My life is here in Stonebrook. It always has been, and it always will be."

He takes a slow step backward. Without another word, I get in the car and drive away. This whole time of doing the dating experiment, I'd been focused on the wrong thing. I wanted to feel fireworks. I wanted the thrill and excitement and cupid arrows and heart-eye emojis. It never occurred to me that the good parts are just half the equation.

The other half is heartbreak.

CHAPTER TWENTY-SEVEN

The glow of my television turns the whole room a teal-green hue. I guess the Hulu app got tired of waiting for me to choose something to watch, and now it's just blaring its logo at me hoping I'll press a button already. I look idly over at the remote, then push the middle circle button. The teal-green disappears and a random show begins. The theme song is too cheerful, too upbeat.

I'd rather watch nothing than listen to this family-friendly happy show, but I'm too tired to turn it off. I'm not tired in a sleepy sense, because I've been sleeping all day. I'm tired mentally, exhausted to my core. I can feel it in my bones and no amount of sleep can drag it out of me. Exhaustion has wholly taken over me in the last week.

Luca hasn't been to school all week because of his concussion, but there's only one more week of school left and all his teachers have agreed that his grades are good enough to skip the final exams. I wish I could skip the next week too, but they don't give out medical excuses for being an idiot. So instead of skipping school, I've just skipped the last two STEM Club meetings. I am a coward.

I almost fall back asleep but a knock at my door wakes me up. "Are you decent?"

"Yeah," I call back, rolling over on my side to face the door. "Since when do you ask if I'm decent?" Luca always just barges right in. At least he used to.

"Dang." He's all smirky-normal-Luca when we slips into my bedroom, closing the door behind him. His bruising and scratches have healed a lot in the past week. He got his temporary cast replaced with a maroon and white hard cast, the colors of our college. When he got out of the hospital, he shaved the rest of his head to match the part with staples. He's already looking close to normal.

I roll my eyes. "It's not like you haven't seen it all before."

"That's why it's disappointing to walk in here when you're fully clothed." He sits on my bed. "It's a total let down."

I roll my eyes again and throw in a sigh for good measure. "What's up?"

"I think we should have a State of the Relationship meeting."

I quirk an eyebrow, but that's actually a good idea. "I have something to say first."

"Oh?" He crosses his legs and rests his broken arm on his knee.

"I didn't accept FLU. I'm going to A&M."

"Seriously?" he says, breaking to a wide grin. "Honey, that's amazing."

His reaction makes me smile too. Luca loves me. Maybe I was wrong in trying to give all of this up for a college far away. I ignore the pain in my chest. "What did you want to talk about?"

"We graduate next week. How many dates have you been on?" Luca asks, his voice taking a serious tone like we're coworkers and these five dates are just a sales quota. He only makes eye contact for a second before looking down. His finger traces the cat pattern on my comforter.

"How many dates have *you* been on?"

"Four," Luca says.

"Just four?" I picture the white sundress girl and the feeling in my stomach when I saw her kiss him. That feeling multiplies four more times, twisting my gut into painful knots for each date he went on. *This is what I wanted,* I remind myself. Why does the idea of Luca being with other girls make me feel so sick inside?

"Your turn," he says, his gaze flitting to mine for a split second before he focuses back on the comforter. "How many?"

"Four."

He looks relieved. "Perfect."

"How so?"

He turns to face me, our knees touching. He takes my hands in his, running his thumbs over my palms. It feels weirdly intimate sitting here so close to him. A tingle flickers in my belly when those dark blue eyes meet mine.

"Be my fifth date," he says, squeezing my hands. "Go out with me tonight."

That is the last thing I expected to hear. "We can't do that. It's supposed to be five different people."

He shakes his head. "We can do whatever we want. The study said people find their soulmate after five relationships... well I want you to be my fifth. And I want to be yours."

"Luca..." I slide my hands out of his. "Do you think going on a date will magically make us soulmates?"

"Of course not. You're already my soulmate. I'm just going to prove it to you."

He still doesn't know I saw the girl in the hospital. "You mean to tell me that in all four of your dates, none of them meant anything? No one sparked any *feelings?*"

"Those dates were just dates. Me and you… we're the real deal."

"Really?" I fold my arms over my chest. "That girl who kissed you in the hospital meant nothing to you?"

His eyebrows shoot up. "How did you—"

"Wrong place, wrong time," I say.

"Honey…" Luca reaches for my hand again. "Please go on a date with me."

It kills me that he's not elaborating. Who is that girl? Why did she call him baby?

My heart feels squeezed in a vice. This right here, me and Luca, together like old times, is so easy. It's natural. I want to believe him, but I know what I saw in that hospital room. "You really think we're soulmates?"

"I know it," he says softly. "Don't you?"

I go quiet for a long time. I got jealous as hell seeing him kiss another girl but does jealousy mean our souls are meant to be together for all of eternity? Being around Luca doesn't feel like it feels when I'm around Mason. But Mason is going off to college. Whatever feelings my heart had for him no longer matters.

"I don't know," I say finally. If I could flip a switch and feel for Luca the way I felt about Mason that night at the museum, everything would be perfect.

"Will you go out with me tonight?"

I look him in the eyes, see the heartache and hope and pure kindness that is Luca staring back at me. He's my best friend. My oldest friend. Family. Maybe that's worth more than being soulmates. I nod. "Okay."

"Thank you," he says, leaning forward and kissing my forehead. "Thank you, babe. Get dressed. I have the best night planned for us."

Luca's brand new truck smells like luxury. I marvel at the soft leather seats and the fancy touch screen in the dash. Insurance only paid out enough for the down payment, but Luca swears he'll make plenty of money working at R&B now that we're almost graduated and he can work full time around college classes.

I wonder what my life would have been like if I had just ignored the desire to apply to FLU. Luca and I would still be together now, and we'd probably still be going out on a date tonight, and exactly nothing in my life would be different.

The weight of that realization takes a minute to sink in, and when it does I am overcome with a certain anxiety I have never felt before.

Does Mason's existence not matter?

Does missing my college acceptance date not matter?

Does anything matter outside of this small town and my high school sweetheart? If it's all going to end up the same anyway, why did I even bother to have these dreams of something new and different?

Luca pulls into a neighborhood called Lakewood Grove. It's an older subdivision with houses built around a small retention pond that's been set up to look like a lake. Almost every home here has been for sale at some point in my life, and the moms are most likely the people who sold them to the next resident.

"Why are we here?" I ask, figuring Luca needs to make a detour to one of the R&B projects and drop off or pick up something for the dads. "Work stuff?"

"Sort of," he says, flashing me a grin. He turns to the left, down Shady Willow Lane, and memories flood back to me. This is the street where the dads renovated a home one summer. Since school was out and the moms were busy at the office, Luca and I hung out on the jobsites a lot, playing and climbing trees and making friends with the neighborhood kids. We must have played in the front yards of two dozen houses over the summers as children, but this one yard that Luca stops in front of is a yard I'll never forget.

That tree, the large oak with branches that spread out far and wide, is the exact same tree where it happened. We were twelve years old, and it was a long, long time coming. The moms constantly joked that we'd get married someday. Our teachers did, too. All the kids in school would call us boyfriend and girlfriend, but in that teasing mocking way that kids do when they still think the opposite sex has cooties.

Luca had climbed the knobby branches way up high, higher than I would dare to go. He called up to me, urging me to join him so I could see the view. I made it up two branches, about seven feet above the ground, and I froze. There was no way in hell I was going to climb up there to meet him. Nope.

So he climbed back down to me and held my hand and said it was okay. And that's when it happened.

Our first kiss.

Luca cuts the engine. Warm feelings of nostalgia flood the cab of the truck and I peer at him, a soft smile pressing against my lips. "Our tree," I murmur.

He nods. "I knew you'd remember."

I grin. "That's sweet but... we can't just trespass on someone's front lawn."

Luca's eyes sparkle mischievously, and I know that's exactly what he plans to do. "Yes we can," he says, and then he's out of the truck, running up to the tree before I can yell at him to stay.

I hastily climb out of the truck and rush up to him, looking around for signs that someone is watching us from a neighboring window. "Luca!" I whisper-yell. "Get out of their yard."

"It's my yard," he says, throwing his free arm up and turning around in a circle. When he stops, he looks at me with the biggest grin. "*Our* yard."

That's when I notice the R&B Realty sign in the front yard, the SOLD placard stuck on top of it. The lights are off and there are no cars in the driveway, so the house must be vacant.

"What are you saying?"

Luca wets his lips and then gnaws on the bottom one. "Well... it was a foreclosure. The company bought it and the dads were going to fix it up and flip it."

I stare at him, waiting for the rest of the story.

Luca draws in a deep breath. "When I realized which house it was—I knew it was fate. That's our tree. And this should be our house. I talked the dads into letting me buy it."

"*What?*" The word tumbles out of me in shock. Working part time at R&B only pays so much and Luca spends most of that on gas, food, and video games. "You don't have any money to buy a house."

Luca nods. "Not now... but someday. The dads already paid for it. They got a great deal. It's livable right now, but it needs work. I'm going to do all the labor myself and buy the materials at cost. All we have to pay is the taxes and insurance after graduation. And then one day, when we can afford it, the dads will sell it back to us for what they paid."

I gaze up at the one-story brick home. It has a large porch, and a high-peak roof, and an attached garage. There's a big back yard, too. It's not a bad house. It's actually kind of great.

"You bought us a house," I say, testing the words on my tongue. "You bought us a *house*?"

Luca steps forward and takes my hands in his. His forehead lowers to mine. "You're my soulmate, Honey Blackwell. You always have been, and you always will be. I want to be with you for the rest of my life. I love you."

"I love you," I breathe, closing my eyes as I lean into Luca's strong, familiar chest. His good arm wraps around me, and his chin rests on top of my head, cocooning me in his embrace. I breathe him in, the scent of his Coolwater cologne, that cinnamon smell in his hair. This feels right.

It must have been senior-year cold feet. Or a temporary lapse in sanity. It was something that knocked me off my orbit, made me think I wanted something different from this life. Science isn't love. Science measures in absolutes, not intangible emotions. That study I found online can only measure a handful of facts, but it doesn't know everything. I didn't need five dates to figure out who my soulmate was, because I've known my soulmate my whole life. My parents were the exception. Luca's parents were the exception.

Maybe we're the exception too.

CHAPTER TWENTY-EIGHT

The R&B event hall is lit up like the Vegas strip. At the hands
of the moms, the large, industrial barn-shaped building has
been transformed from its usual warehouse into a beautiful,
sparkling graduation party for the Stonebrook High senior
class. Music pumps through the speakers behind Nate Garcia,
a junior on the track team who was hired to be the DJ for
tonight. Luca said he was pretty psyched that the moms gave
him the gig because it's the first time he's been paid for his
self-taught DJ skills.

Luca's hand wraps around mine, our fingers laced together
just like old times as we enter the party. Luca is still wearing
his silver graduation cap, but I left mine back at home,
choosing instead to wear the pale blue sequined dress I had
on under my gown. In a way, this our coming out party. Or
our "getting back together" party. With Luca missing school,
the hallways haven't seen us back together yet.

Graduation was fun, and it took hardly no time at all.
When your senior class is just under two hundred people, the
event isn't much of a spectacle. Maggie gave a kickass saluta-

torian speech and then before I knew it, we were all filing out of the school auditorium for the very last time. Surreal doesn't even describe the feeling of being completely finished with high school. I try to put the thought out of my mind because every time I think about the future, I think of my dream college, and how I'll never get to go. It feels like I've been sucker-punched in the gut.

Across the room, I see the moms chatting with Ms. Bodhi, the art teacher. Jill sees me and waves. I wave back, wincing as I take a step forward and these stupid heels dig into my feet. I'd bought the shoes at a cheap shoe store because they matched my dress but wearing them to graduation was a bad idea. If I take them off, the blisters will make my feet look like a murder scene.

"Let's go say hi before we socialize," Luca says, spotting the moms at the same time I do.

We make our way over there. Jill looks gorgeous in a skintight, golden gown that's probably not appropriate for a high school graduation party. But she rocks it anyhow. My mom is wearing the black dress she wears to every event that requires a dress. Her hair is pulled high in a sleek ponytail, and she wears those drop diamond earrings my dad gave her years ago.

"Would you look at our graduates!" Jill says, beaming at us. "All grown up." She wraps her son in a bear hug, despite the fact that he towers over her.

Mom smiles at me, a soft, half-sad expression that I can only imagine is filled with motherly thoughts of her precious kid being an adult now. At least, that's what she's thinking if she's anything like Jill. When she pulls me into a hug, I see the dark circles under her eyes. She's been staying up late watching TV in the guest bedroom for weeks now. I wonder if me graduating is taking such a toll on her, or if it's something else. Maybe the business isn't doing as well as the dads act like it is.

When Mom releases me, Jill pulls me in for a hug, nearly squeezing my lungs out. "What do you think about the party?" she asks.

"It looks great."

Luca nods. "You really outdid yourself this year."

Jill looks at my mom and smiles. "I've been saying we should use this venue as, well, a venue! Not just a stuffy old warehouse that sits here and costs money to maintain. We should start renting it out for parties, weddings, all kinds of stuff."

The moment she says the W-word, I feel her eyes lock on mine. Sure enough, she's beaming at me. "This place would make a great wedding venue… maybe even for two lovebirds I happen to know?" She gives us an exaggerated wink. My stomach lurches.

Luca and I are back together, but the idea of marriage is a mountain I haven't yet mentally tackled. I love Luca. I'm going to be with him forever. But I'm not sure I'm ready to go walking down a rustic warehouse aisle and making lifelong vows anytime soon.

"Oh, stop it," Mom tells her best friend. "Let the kids take their time."

I give her a grateful smile, but Mom has turned her attention to the soda in her hand. She tosses her head back and takes a long sip, almost like she wishes it was alcohol.

"You kids go have fun," Jill says. "We'll be back around midnight to lock up."

I cling to Luca's elbow as we walk around and mingle with friends, hugging and saying our goodbyes to those lucky graduates who are getting out of Stonebrook and going off to college in the fall. My feet are killing me, and I hope that holding onto my boyfriend will somehow help levitate me off the floor, but it doesn't.

"Have you seen Maggie?" I ask Luca.

He shakes his head. "I don't think so."

I take another look around the room. It's large and filled with people, but if my best friend were here, I'd have seen her by now. "She should be here. I'm going to call her." Seizing my opportunity to sit down and let my feet rest, I rush over to one of the white folding chairs that line the walls and take my phone out of my clutch.

The music must be too loud in here because I totally didn't hear the three missed calls from Maggie. I skim her texts and realize her car battery died and her parents are out so she's stranded at home, unable to come to the party.

I'm on my way to get you, I text back.

I peel off my shoes and wince at the large blisters on my heels, toes, and even on the side of my foot. The warehouse floor is not a place for bare feet, or maybe I'd just kick off these shoes and go barefoot for the rest of the night. I look out at the old, painted concrete floor and curl my lip. Not happening. Plus, with all of these blisters, they're probably just waiting to get infected if I step on something gross.

With a sigh of defeat, I slide the wretched things back onto my feet and force myself to stand. I wish I knew who invented high heels so I could go back in time and slap them. Or, even better—go back in time and prevent them from ever inventing such a horrible shoe. Then I could save all of humanity from being subjected to these things.

I hobble around until I find Luca standing with his track buddies. Shawn Beck looks adorable tonight in black slacks and an emerald green dress shirt that matches his eyes. Maggie simply cannot miss out on this.

"Hey, Shawn," I say. "You're single, right?"

"Single as a Pringle," Shawn says with a dorky wink that does not fit his popular persona.

"Okay, maybe saying things like that is why you're single."

"Um, excuse you," Luca says, sliding his arm around my waist. "Why is my girlfriend asking that?"

I roll my eyes. "Maybe my friend has a slight crush on him."

"Wait," Shawn says. "Which friend? Is she here?" His head spins on a swivel. "You have to introduce me."

"I'm thinking about it," I admit. "Her name is Maggie Sinclair."

"That hot British girl?" Shawn says, putting a hand on his chest. "Hell yes."

Maggie's crush on Shawn has only grown over senior year, to the point where she's entirely too scared to ask him out. Maybe I can make some magic happen on this graduation night. Even better if I can embarrass her the way she embarrassed me in front of Mason.

I turn to Luca. "Maggie's car broke down and she's stranded at her house. We need to go get her."

He hesitates, his gaze dropping to the blue plastic cup in his hand. "Er... not a good idea, babe. I don't *think* I'm drunk yet but—"

"Yet?" My lips press together. "You're drinking? You have a concussion. Plus, this is kind of the whole idea of the Project Graduation party!" It's supposed to stop teens from drinking by giving them something fun and sober to do. The moms would be pissed if they knew Luca and his friends snuck alcohol into this thing.

"Babe, it's graduation," he says, making the last word have four, long drawn-out syllables. I don't know why I'm so surprised. Of course he'd drink tonight. I bet a ton of people will be secretly drinking. I'm annoyed despite the facts. I'm trying so hard here, working my emotions on overdrive to keep all my negative thoughts contained far, far away from my relationship. And then Luca does crap like this and makes it really hard to let it go.

"We can't leave her at home, Luca. She's my best friend. She should be here."

He reaches into his pocket and hands me the keys to his brand new truck. I'm surprised he's letting me drive it. "Go get her and then we can party together."

I take the keys and turn sharply around, intent on storming out of this place. My feet, however, have different plans. I wince and hobble toward the doors, carrying myself on blistered feet until I finally get to Luca's truck. I pull off the heels and toss them in the backseat, vowing that I'll never wear them again.

Relief washes over me now that my bare feet can finally breathe. I'm eager to celebrate this night with my best friend and hook her up with Shawn. If anything will take my mind off being annoyed with Luca drinking, it'll be seeing Maggie finally get a date with her crush. But first, I need better shoes.

Stopping at my house, I park on the side of the road so I don't have to maneuver Luca's massive truck around my dad's truck in our driveway. Feeling like a weirdo in a fancy dress with no shoes on, I quickly rush up the sidewalk and let myself inside.

The living room is dark, but a light pours into the hallway from Dad's office. He must be working from home, even though it's a Friday night. One of these days, my parents need to learn how to take a break. I make my way upstairs and find a pair of ballet flats, then I slip into the bathroom and grab a handful of bandages. Covering all the blisters in a thick layer of first aid supplies, I try on the flats and stand up.

It's not exactly like walking on clouds, but I can manage. I might even be able to pull off a few moves on the dance floor if the bandages stay in place.

The floor rumbles beneath my bandaged feet, which means the garage door is opening. If Dad is going back to work, I'll have to yell at him for never taking a break. I head downstairs, stopping halfway when I hear Mom's voice.

"I can't do this anymore," she says—practically shouts—from the foyer. "Blaine, I just can't."

"It's just a few more weeks until they start college," Dad says. "They'll probably move into their house soon."

A sharp knot forms in my stomach. The thudding of my heart in my chest is like a warning bell, telling me to turn around and run upstairs so I don't hear anything else.

My heart's good intentions are futile. I stay right here, a few steps from the second floor landing, listing to my parents talk.

"This is too hard. I'm tired of pretending."

"Amber," Dad says in an exhausted tone that tells me this isn't the first time they've talked about it.

Talked about *what*, though? What the hell am I overhearing?

"I filed for divorce," Mom says.

The world drops out from under my feet.

"Dammit, Amber. We agreed to wait."

I step carefully down the stairs and round the banister before they even notice I'm here.

"Honey!" Dad holds up his hand, almost as if he thinks the

motion will somehow stop me from hearing, seeing, or remembering what's happening. "When did you get here?"

His voice is unnervingly calm.

That only pisses me off more.

"You're getting a divorce?" I say. It's a miracle the words even come out right because I have never, ever, even so much as thought those words before. I glance at Mom, still in her black dress, her eye makeup a little smudged.

She stares right back at me but doesn't say anything.

"Let's sit down and talk about this," Dad says. He seems so cool and collected, as if he knew this would happen some-day. As if he has rehearsed this day a million times.

"I'm not going to *sit down*," I say, my voice broken and weak and going in a million directions. "You don't love each other anymore?"

"Of course we love each other," Dad says swiftly. I'm sure that's another one of his rehearsed lines. He glances at Mom. "We've just grown apart."

She nods, finally finding her voice. "We fell in love in high school but then we grew up and became different people."

"But you're soulmates."

"We were waiting until you graduated to tell you." Dad rubs his brow, conveniently not acknowledging what I said. "We didn't want to upset you."

"I didn't ask you to stay together." I bite out the words over the hollow feeling in my chest. This is wrong. It can't be happening.

"I know, I know. But we wanted to, Honey. We didn't want to break up in your senior year. We didn't want to worry you or Luca."

"Don't make yourself unhappy for my sake!" I am full on crying now.

"It's not just that." Dad sighs. "Your mom and I have a reputation. We're the *high school sweethearts*, same as Luca's parents. If we split up, it'll be a town scandal. It'll hurt the business. We've just been waiting for the right time."

This stupid business. Everything is for the business.

A horrible thought wedges in my throat. "And Luca's parents?"

"They're fine," Dad says. "Well, as far as I know, they're fine. They're happy."

"Do they know?" I ask.

Dad actually looks remorseful, and I'm not sure if it's part of his script or if he's truly feeling as bad as he should feel about this. "They don't know."

It all hits me now. Mom, staying up late watching TV in the guest room. Mom, with dark circles under her eyes and her desire to focus only on work and nothing else. She's already left Dad in her mind, just not on paper.

"Honey, let's talk," Dad says. His entire face is made of fine lines that press together, his mouth just one big frown.

I stand up and hold tightly to Luca's truck key as I stare down at my dad from the stairs. He's one of the people in this world that I thought I could trust, could count on. Completely and wholly, forever and ever. He's my dad. But I was wrong about that, and maybe I've been wrong about other things.

"I have no desire to talk." With that, I turn and walk out to Luca's truck, not feeling the pain in my feet. Not feeling much of anything. If my parents' perfect relationship was only smoke and mirrors, then maybe mine is too.

CHAPTER TWENTY-NINE

"Oh, my god."

I haven't been counting, but this is at least the tenth time Maggie has uttered those words since I showed up at her door twenty minutes ago.

"How is this my life?" I say while staring at her ceiling from my place on the floor of her bedroom. "How in the hell is this real?"

"Now I know why you never showed up last night."

After the nightmare of last night, I had left Luca's truck parked in front of my house and cried myself to sleep on his bed. He didn't stumble home until two in the morning, where he promptly fell asleep next to me without even asking why I never returned to the party. On any other occasion, I'd be pissed. But I don't care about Luca's bad boyfriend antics right now.

"I'm sorry," I say, frowning at her. "I should have told you." Maggie sits on the floor too, organizing her eyeshadow palettes next to me. "I meant to text you. I just—I just broke. I couldn't do anything. And Luca's drunk ass didn't even realize I never came back to the party."

"He is a fun drunk," she says in this weird way.

I sit up on my elbow. "How do you know?"

She gives me a wry smile. "I ended up at the grad party, after all. Shawn picked me up. Well—he got an Uber and picked me up."

I sit all the way up. "And you're only telling me this now?"

She shrugs. "You had epic news. I only have silly girl-crush news. It can wait."

"Details," I say, brushing the hair from my face. Every inch of my body is still angry, betrayed, and hurt, but I need something else to focus on right now.

"I don't have many details… not yet, at least. Shawn heard you talking about me and I guess he wondered where I was, so he got my number from Luca and texted me. Then we went to the party but he was already kind of drunk so we just danced and hung out. But…" She bats her false eyelashes at me. "We're going on a date next week."

"Finally!" I hold up my hand and she smacks me with a high-five. "I'm so sorry I wasn't there."

"It's probably for the best. I would have been too shy and just clung to you all night. But you weren't there and I had to step out of my comfort zone."

"I'm happy for you, Mags."

It shouldn't be so hard to summon genuine excitement for my best friend, but the struggle is real. I can't shake the thoughts from my head. The realization of my parents living a lie, the memories of my mom's epic bad mood lately. She's heartbroken. He's moving on. My parent's happy relationship fell apart and I didn't even realize it.

Maybe it's because they've only ever been with each other. My parents didn't take a break and date other people like Luca and I did. Maybe that's what broke them apart, the question that maybe someone else is out there and that person is a better match.

I hold onto this hope, telling myself that Luca and I will be fine. That staying together isn't a huge mistake.

"Maybe you should talk to him," Maggie says softly.

"Huh?" I look up at her.

She's giving me a pitying look. "The wheels in your brain are clearly turning on overdrive. Go talk to him, love. Figure out your shite instead of dwelling on your parents'."

"Do I really want to be with him?" I ask, each word a sharp stabby betrayal in my gut. "Because I'm not sure he's my soul-mate. And I don't want to be like my parents eighteen years from now." I grab the sides of my head and curl my fists into my hair. "Or maybe I'm just overthinking everything. Maybe Luca and I are fine."

But if we are fine, why do I still long for Mason to text me?

Maggie gives me a safe look that doesn't reveal her true thoughts. "That's up to you, Hon. You need to talk to him. Figure it out."

I push myself up on my elbows. "I guess it won't hurt to try."

Luca is snoring so loudly I wouldn't be surprised if the walls started rumbling. For a brief moment, I can almost picture myself waking up in the master bedroom of the house on Shady Willow Lane, Luca snoring obnoxiously next to me.

Is this what I want for the rest of my life?

I lie down next to him on top of his sheets. I tuck my arm under a pillow and turn on my side, staring at Luca as if I'm examining him for the first time.

He blinks awake. "Hey," he says, a sleepy smile on his face.

"You hungover?" I ask.

I can count the number of times Luca has been drunk on one hand. I was there for all of them, until last night. Each morning he woke up sick as hell, vowing to never drink again. If he's in the same state of hungover misery this morning, I won't be able to talk to him.

"Nah," he says, reaching over and brushing my hair behind my ear. "I didn't drink too much after you left. Why didn't you come back?"

"It's a really long story."

"Everything okay?"

Funny how my head automatically wants to nod yes, to assure him that everything is fine. I stop myself. Everything is not fine.

"No," I say. "It's about my parents."

Luca's worry falls right off his face. He yawns and rolls over onto his back. His phone vibrates and he checks it, typing out a quick reply.

"It's about my parents but it affects us," I clarify, waiting for him to finish texting.

His brow lifts in my direction. "What do your parents have to do with us?"

A quick *tap, tap* on Luca's door ruins the moment. "Good morning," Jill sing-songs from the other side of the door. "It's almost lunchtime, kiddos. Got the grill all fired up but it looks like it's going to rain soon so hurry up. Don't be late!"

I groan internally. I haven't been hungry since I discovered my parent's secret.

"Oh hell yes, a burger sounds amazing," Luca says, sitting up quickly in bed and smashing a kiss to my forehead. "Can we talk later?"

"Sure," I say, offering him a small smile. It's only the most devastating news of my life. It can totally wait.

CHAPTER THIRTY

My dad laughs. A deep, belly rumble of happiness. He flips a burger on the grill. Takes a sip of beer, then throws out a joke to his best friend.

How can he stand here and act normal? How can he grill burgers and hang out and laugh act like every bit of his life isn't a lie?

I glance over at my mom, who is two glasses of wine into the afternoon. She's sitting on the swing next to Jill and she looks normal too, at least on the surface. Now that I *know*, it's impossible to miss the signs. Mom's drinking, keeping to her quiet demeanor that's developed over the last year or two. Dad is joking and having loud, boisterous fun with his best friend, acting as if everything is okay. Acting as if he's a carefree bachelor.

Their life is a lie.

My life has been pulled into their lie.

I can't take it anymore. I have known about my parent's secret life for less than twenty four hours and yet I can't take it. "Luca," I say, tugging on his arm. "I have to show you something in my room."

"Sure, can it wait a minute?" He's holding an empty plate in front of my dad, waiting for his burger to finish cooking. His phone is in his other hand. I'm guessing he's getting a million texts about the party last night because he's normally not on it as much. Or maybe it's that girl in the white dress.

"No."

Luca relents, setting the paper plate back on top of the stack. Dad doesn't even look my way; he's oblivious that anything is wrong.

"What is it?" Luca asks, following me inside.

"I can't talk in here," I say, looking around. We go to my room and I close the door behind us.

"You are being exceptionally weird," Luca says. His phone vibrates loudly in his pocket.

I turn to face him, my fingers twisting together in front of me. There's no proper way to say it, so I just say it. "My parents are getting divorced."

"Holy shit!" Luca's eyes are wild with the juicy gossip. "No way!"

Tears flood my vision. "This isn't funny."

"Baby, I'm not laughing." Luca grabs my arms and pulls me against his chest. "Don't cry. I'm just...wow... this crazy news. I didn't expect it."

That only makes me cry harder. "You don't get it," I say, pushing away from him as I wipe my eyes. "My parents don't love each other. They aren't soulmates."

Luca frowns. "Honey... they aren't us."

"Yes, they are! Don't you get it? They were high school sweethearts. They are exactly us and they failed. If they can't make it work, what makes you think we can?"

"Well, for starters… my parents," Luca says. "They are still together."

"We don't know that for a fact." I hate myself for even hinting that Jill and Tony are lying to him the same way my parents lied to me. But for all I know, maybe everyone in this entire world is just one huge liar.

Luca's lips press into a thin line. "We're not like your parents. And we're not like my parents."

"How?" I say, throwing my arms in the air. "How are we different? We are genetically like them. We were raised by them. We were shoved into their little mold of what they think we should be. We only ever had each other to date and we thought we'd grow up to be just like them, and guess what? I don't want to be like my parents, Luca. I don't want to be living a lie just for the sake of what people will think of us."

"We aren't like them," Luca says, his voice stronger now. "Honey, listen to me."

I stop pacing the length of my room and fold my hands over my chest. My breath is deep and ragged, but I look into his dark blue eyes and try to trust the boy I've known my whole life. "How do you know we'll be different?"

His phone vibrates in his pocket.

That's when I see it.

It's nearly invisible—that little twitch of longing in his eyes—the imperceptible surprise and fervent jolt he felt when his phone got a new text. But all of Luca's invisible body language is perfectly visible to me. I know him as well as I know myself. Maybe even better.

I take a step back. Wipe off the remaining tears on my cheeks. Swallow the lump in my throat.

"Luca, who is texting you?"

"Huh?" He shrugs. Tosses his phone onto the bed without looking at it. "Nothing. No one. I'm here for *you*, Honey. No one else."

I tilt my head. "It's her, isn't it? Hospital girl?"

The look on his face tells me everything.

I laugh. "Is she your soulmate?"

"What?" He flinches, squishes up his face in denial. "No. You're my soulmate, Honey. I choose you."

I'm still laughing, albeit a bit deliriously. I shake my head. "No, Luca. You don't get it. You're not supposed to *choose* me. It's just supposed to *be* me. And if it's not me, then…" I lift my hands and shrug. "Maybe it's her."

Luca blinks, his gaze dropping to the floor. After a long moment, he says, "Her name is Robyn. We met in Apple Valley."

"You like her," I say softly.

He nods. When he looks up, his eyes are bloodshot. Tears pool in the corners. "I'm so sorry, Honey. I'm sorry. I didn't mean to fall for someone else, I—"

I step closer, putting a hand on his chest. "Don't apologize. I think I did the same thing…"

"You met someone else?" He seems more relieved than jealous. And oddly, I'm also more relieved than jealous. I'm not even sure I'm jealous at all.

"I think so," I answer honestly. "I mean, maybe not. I can't stop thinking about him."

He grins. "It's weird, huh?"

"Very weird."

I reach out with both of my hands. He grabs onto them and we stand here face to face, hands clasped, just like old times. I peer up at him. "If you feel this way about Robyn, why are you staying with me?"

"I guess it seems like the right thing to do."

"For the business," I say.

"For the family," he says.

"Because everyone expects it."

"Because it's familiar."

"And easy," I say.

I squeeze his hands. He squeezes back. I see that little scar on his lip. "I love you, Luca," I say, exhaling. "But I don't think we're in love."

He shakes his head. "I don't think we are."

We stand here another long moment, alone with our thoughts, with the truth, which inflates until it fills up every inch of my bedroom. Which one of us is going to say it first?

I'll do it. "Are we breaking up for good this time?"

"I think we are," he says, his voice gravely and raw.

I nod. He pulls me closer, wrapping his arms around me. I lean against him, tucking my cheek right against his neck where it always goes, but this time it feels different. He still feels like home, but different somehow. Like when you're digging through the back of the closet and come across a box of beloved old toys. I can't throw out Luca, but I also don't want to lose him.

"Friends?" I ask as I break away from our hug.

"Oh yeah," he says, nodding. "Always."

CHAPTER THIRTY-ONE

While everyone else relishes in the newfound freedom of summer vacation after graduation, I'm wishing I still had the comfort of going to school. I spent all those years dreading the alarm clock each day, enduring countless annoying bus rides until Luca got a car, and wasting so many hours on homework. My mandatory public school education is finally over and here I am wishing I could go back.

Right now all I do is work at R&B and watch Maggie get ready for New York. When my freshman year of college starts, I won't be living on campus, so I don't even have to show up at the school until my first day in August.

It's all so dreadfully mundane.

There are no freshman traditions at A&M. I won't have a dorm room to decorate with cute stuff from Target, or a view of the mountains to keep me company during my studies. Going to A&M requires driving to class, then coming home. It'll be easy. And simple. And exactly what my parents want.

I stare at the moonstone ring on my nightstand. My index finger has a smooth crease all the way around it from where the ring has lived for the last five years. I never took it off. Not until Luca and I officially broke up. Now it just feels weird to wear jewelry from my ex. It also feels weird not to wear it. I keep touching my finger with my thumb, muscle memory making me want to spin the ring around. Every time my thumb touches flesh instead of silver, I feel thrown off my axis.

Maggie says it'll just take time to get over the mental trauma of breaking up with Luca, and that *time heals all wounds* and that maybe I should do some epic cathartic thing to rid him from my system. I say time can't possibly heal *all* wounds. Time won't heal a gunshot blast to the chest. And it sure as hell won't erase eighteen years of memories.

The cathartic thing might help a teensy bit. But I can't exactly burn an effigy of my relationship with Luca. It's not just this moonstone ring that would need to go up in flames. I'd have to burn the entire house down. Every memory I have, every outfit I own, every single item in my bedroom—they all have some connection with Luca Rollins. I wonder if Mom feels the same way about Dad.

Maybe setting fire to the place actually would be therapeutic. But it's also illegal.

I clear the thought from my mind and turn over in my bed. I've almost stopped thinking about Mason constantly. Now I only think about him a few times a day. I'm not allowing myself to waste time daydreaming about what could have been at my dream college, and I certainly can't waste time thinking about committing arson. All that's left to do is move forward.

My phone screen lights up.

>**Mason (like the jar):** So I'm trying this new
>science experiment…

What the crap? I haven't heard from him since I rushed out of his house after being a complete bitch to him. I didn't even see him at graduation. Now he's just texting me like nothing happened? Mason is the chilliest person on the planet.

I know I need to move forward and accept my new life as a single woman living in Stonebrook, getting a boring business degree.

Texting with Mason is not moving forward.

But facts and logic won't stop me from replying.

>**Me:** Oh yeah? What is it?
>**Mason (like the jar):** It's where I text girls to
>apologize for being a sexist ass who assumed
>they made decisions solely because of guys.
>To begin my experiment, I'd like to apologize
>to you. It was shitty of me and I'm sorry.
>**Me:** What is your hypothesis?
>**Mason (like the jar):** Hypothesis is that I may
>not be forgiven, but it's worth it to try.
>**Me:** And how many girls are a part of the
>experiment?
>**Mason (like the jar):** Just one.
>**Me:** That's not a very big control group.
>**Mason (like the jar):** Which really sucks
>because the results are incredibly important
>to me.
>**Me:** Shall I provide my data now?
>**Mason (like the jar):** Please.

Me: You're forgiven.

Mason (like the jar): Looks like the experiment
is a resounding success.

I wish I could tell him how much I'm giggling over here. How light it makes me feel to text with him again. Instead I just send him a thumbs up emoji.

While I'm thinking about things I wish I could say, several more things come to mind. Like how I wish Mason and I had been actual friends all these years instead of enemies. Or maybe more than friends. How I want to tell him everything with my screwed up parents and how I'm not over him and I don't know if I ever will be. How I wish I'd never met him. How I wish I could kiss him again.

Mostly, I wish I could tell him I'll see him on the first day of college.

***

The TV in the guest bedroom turns off, flooding the hallway in darkness. I check the time on my phone—three-fifteen in the morning. Mom's soft footsteps venture down the hallway and soon she's at my door. My heart lurches in my throat. We've barely spoken since graduation. That was a week ago.

"Yes?" I say after an uncomfortable fifteen seconds of her standing in the doorway.

"Can I come in?" Mom asks.

I shrug, my eyes on my laptop, which is playing a show I've seen a million times. "It's your house."

Mom enters slowly, looking around my room as if she's never seen it before. Then she sits on my bed. I don't think she's been in here all school year. Maybe not even in two years. Mom is always busy with work and she spends most of her free time hanging out with Jill or Aunt Bree. We haven't spent much time alone together since I was in junior high. I spent all this time thinking she was cold and mean and that Jill was a better mom. When really my mom was just hurting. A better daughter would have noticed this. But I was too busy fighting with my heart and worrying about myself to see anyone else's pain.

"I love this show," Mom says, laying down next to me. I turn the laptop screen so we can both see it. We watch an entire episode in silence, despite the fact that this show has won tons of comedy awards.

When the opening song starts on new episode, I hear her sniffle.

My mom is crying. I look over. "Mom?"

Her dark eyes meet mine and she brings two fingers up under her eyes, deftly wiping away the evidence. "I'm sorry."

"It's... fine," I say after a moment. I know it's not fine because my mom is crying on my bed and my heart is breaking for her. "I'm here if you want to talk," I manage to stutter out, knowing how awkward all of it is. Kids aren't supposed to play therapist to their parents.

Mom wipes her eyes again. "I talked to Bree."

I shift up on my elbow and peer at her. "What does she think about all of this?"

Aunt Bree is a free spirit, never one to be held down in a relationship.

Mom takes a deep breath. I get the feeling this is one of those moments that defines our new roles as adult parent and adult child. She's no longer wiping baby food off my mouth or gently placing bandages over my scraped knees. We're all grown up now. The look in her eyes tells me she might be thinking the same thing. "Bree is making room for me to stay in her apartment."

I sit up. "You're moving out?"

She nods slowly like she's still making up her mind. "I love your father. I didn't want us to divorce. But he doesn't feel the same way. It's time for me to move on instead of trying to stay here and pretend. You're old enough now to know the truth."

The pain in my mom's eyes is so familiar I can't look away. Mom is heartbroken because the person she loves isn't in love with her anymore. Her life has been shattered, irrevocably changed forever. Her marriage with my dad isn't like an old house; it can't be torn down to the studs and rebuilt better. I think they've finally realized all that's left to do is break out the wrecking ball.

Now I know where I've seen that look before. Mom's eyes carry the same emotions as Luca's had when I first told him we weren't soulmates. That deep, aching sorrow in her gaze is the pain of unrequited love.

"I'm coming with you," I say.

Mom shakes her head. "Absolutely not. This is your home. Bree's place is small, there will barely be enough room for me there."

I heave a sigh, a vision of Aunt Bree's tiny little laundromat apartment in my mind. She's right. I want to go with Mom in solidarity, but the place is too small. "You'll get your own place soon, right?"

Mom nods. "Hopefully. Dad and I are on good terms, Honey. When we divorce, well, we'll still be friends. I'm not leaving the business, and neither will he. We'll just have to find a way to make it work."

"When you get your own place, I'll move in with you," I say, gazing around at my room as if it's already been packed up. I guess in my mind, ever since I found out the truth about my parents, I have mentally wished I was someplace else. "You're hurting and I want to be there for you."

Crap, now I'm all teary-eyed too.

"Don't cry over me," Mom says. "We're all just human, baby. Dad and I were stupid kids and we thought we'd last forever." Her eyes get even sadder. Her lips curl into a frown as she exhales and runs her hand through my hair. "Turns out we were wrong."

CHAPTER THIRTY-TWO

Dad gets up and makes coffee the next morning, taking no cautions to keep the noise down while the rest of us are asleep. He's upset, but Aunt Bree swears he'll come around in time. Despite him trying to talk Mom out of it to keep up appearances with the community, with Luca's parents, and with me, she is moving out today. She's all packed up. Her clothes, and the small essentials she'll take with her to Aunt Bree's until she gets her own place fill just three suitcases. Everything else is going into storage. Dad had argued that she could keep her stuff in the garage, or even still in the house until she gets her own place. That seemed like the practical, frugal option, but Mom refused. I think I know more than anyone that matters of the heart don't always make practical sense. Sometimes you just have to do what you have to do.

I lie awake, Mom sleeping next to me in my bed, and I listen to the sound of my dad banging around the kitchen, and then stomping into the garage. The soft rumble of his truck backs out of the driveway and I listen for the garage door to close all the way, then I sit up and realize Mom is awake, too.

"There are boxes in the garage," she says as if on autopilot as she climbs out of my bed. "Want to help me move stuff to storage?"

All at once everything feels surreal and yet... right. "Of course," I say.

I brew a pot of coffee and Mom dresses into an old pair of workout clothes, her hair pulled into a high ponytail. At first glance, she looks like she might be about to go on an early morning jog with Jill. As I pour our coffees into travel mugs, I imagine an alternate reality where this is just any other regular morning. The daydream comes easily enough, but it doesn't do anything to ease the knot in my chest.

We start with her extra clothes, the non-essential outfits she left out of the suitcases. I fold and tape the bottoms of the boxes, and Mom piles stuff inside, not even trying to keep things organized. Pants and bathing suits and old house slippers all get shoved together and then taped closed. We pack up her knick-knacks and sentimental items that I forgot even existed, and she debates for a long time about the framed photos on the walls, before choosing to take a few of the ones from my childhood. She doesn't take any pictures that have my dad in them.

Mom's eyes are red with dark circles under them, but she doesn't cry.

We carry the boxes out to the driveway. I start loading them into the back of her car. Mom watches me, her hands on her hips, while I shove a box into the trunk, trying to make it fit.

"This will take a lot of trips," she says. "I don't know what I'll do with my furniture. We'll have to borrow a truck from the warehouse or something." She shifts on her feet, then pinches the bridge of her nose. "I can't believe I didn't think this through. Of course I can't move in my car! I need a truck. I need a damned truck."

"Mom, it's okay. We'll figure it out."

"I am such an idiot," she mutters as she shoves a box into her backseat so hard that the edges fold in, bending the box out of shape.

"No you're not," I say, but I'm pretty sure she's not listening.

Luca's truck comes into view at the end of the road. I hadn't even noticed that he wasn't home, that his truck wasn't parked in the same place it always is. We haven't seen each other much since we officially broke up, but we text almost every night.

I know in my heart that I don't want to be with him anymore. He's not my soulmate. I love him. I think part of me always will. It'll be hard going to the same college, taking the same classes, working at the same place. It might be harder to do these things broken up than it would have been to stay together, however unhappy I felt.

I don't think my parents' decision to pretend to still be together all this time was the right thing to do, but I understand it. Right now, I almost wish Luca and I were doing the same kind of acting.

"I need an aspirin," Mom mutters before disappearing into the house.

I kind of want to chase after her just so I don't have to see Luca, but it's too late. My awkward tension fills the air as his truck slows to a stop. He's already seen me standing here with a stupid confused look on my face. Luca doesn't turn into his own driveway. He stops just in front of it. And then his truck backs up, slowly but surely reversing right into my driveway.

He cuts off the engine and climbs out wearing a pair of basketball shorts and an old Stonebrook High Track shirt.

"Luca," I say. "What are you doing here?"

I almost expect him to blush, to say whoops, he accidentally backed into the wrong driveway. Instead, he lowers his tailgate and retrieves a dolly from the bed of his truck. It has the R&B logo on it, and so do the stack of padded furniture blankets that he clearly took from the warehouse at work.

"I'm here to help your mom move."

"You are?" My voice cracks.

He leaves the dolly next to a stack of boxes, then approaches me. My stomach twists into a pretzel as he takes my face in his hands and those eyes I know so well peer into mine. My heart aches in a way I didn't know it could. It would be so easy to wrap my arms around him, to lay my head where it fits perfectly against his chest, and to fall back into what I've always known. Right now, with all of this uncertainty, I almost want to do exactly that.

Luca's lips tip up in a little smile, his hands falling down from my cheeks just seconds after he first put them there. "You were right, Honey. We're not soulmates."

His gaze roams over me, making me feel a little uncomfortable. Like suddenly he can see every little flaw in me, the ones he's ignored all of our lives. But he's smiling, so maybe I'm just imagining that.

"Definitely not soulmates." His hands slip down to mine, our fingers barely touching. "But you are my best friend," he says. "And I'll be here for you every single time you need me. I'll always have your back, Blackwell."

At some point in the last few seconds, my mom came back outside because now Luca looks past me and gives her a friendly smile. "I'm here to help you move."

My eyes flood with grateful tears and I lean up on my toes and wrap my arms around his neck. "Thank you," I breathe against him.

"Thank you," he says, squeezing my hand. "Thanks for fighting for what was right, not what was easy. I'm really sorry you missed out on your college."

I shrug. "It was a stupid idea anyhow."

"No, it's not. Honey, you should go. You should apply again next year."

I swallow. I am not in the mood to delve into this painful subject when I've tried so hard to forget about FLU. "Maybe," I say in the most non-committal way.

"Not maybe. You're going to be an awesome rock doctor."

"Geoscientist," I correct.

He grins, then glances at my mom. "What should I load up first?"

CHAPTER THIRTY-THREE

It's pizza night at the Miller sisters' household. It's still weird thinking of my mom as going by her maiden name, but now that the divorce papers are filed and my parents have agreed to continue running R&B as two separate entities: R&B Construction and R&M Real Estate, this is how things are now. Mom is no longer a Blackwell. She's a Miller.

The new for sale signs look amazing. R&M Real Estate has a brand new logo. Mom and Jill arranged a new photoshoot to get updated pictures taken for their new venture. My mom and her best friend are still standing there, back to back, smiling on their real estate signs, but Mom's not wearing her wedding ring and she has a fresh new haircut.

I wasn't there for the long talks she had with Jill after my parent's relationship imploded, but Mom says Jill is still her best friend, and still supportive of her. As for the rest of our community? We don't know how they'll react to discovering that one half of the legendary High School Sweethearts are done. I guess it doesn't really matter what anyone else thinks.

My parents are putting on a brave face as they move forward, and the Rollins family is still on their side.

I take a step back in someone's front yard, admiring the new sign in the lawn. I've seen the old real estate signs so many times I have that image of Mom and Jill memorized. The old photo didn't do Mom any favors. In baggy dress pants and a blue button up blouse, she looked like a mom who also sold real estate. Mom's new hair, once curly and peppered with gray hair, is a sleek shoulder-length bob that shines under the photography lights. She's wearing a little black dress and bright red high heels. It's not her everyday style, but it looks good. She looks happy. Now, she looks like real estate is lucky to have her.

I'm glad she's able to start her life over and still have her best friend by her side, but I'm not a fan of spending the day driving around to every property they have listed and replacing all the old yard signs with these new ones.

The sun is setting by the time I've finished swapping signs, and now the company van is filled with the old signs, and it smells like dirt and mildew in here. I didn't plan on being a sweat-drenched zombie when I arrived at Aunt Bree's for pizza night with my mom, but these Texas summers are brutal. I don't need an FLU dorm room to know the summers in Colorado are a lot cooler.

I haven't even started A&M yet and I'm already wishing it was next year so I could apply for FLU again. I'm not sure what the process is for applying to a school that accepted you and then you ignored them. There might be some bad blood in the registration process that I need to fix. But for now, I'm still mending a broken heart, getting used to living in my house with only Dad, and trying my hardest to enjoy the single life, like Maggie keeps suggesting.

When I told her she hated "the single life" herself and was over the moon when she and Shawn started dating, well, she had no fancy British comeback for that.

Even though it's hard, I know it's for the best. I am single because I chose to be. I left a good thing behind in search of a great thing. A future. An endless, open canvas of a future that has no parts already colored in. I get to be the artist of my own life from now on.

Aunt Bree's place smells like home, and I'm not sure why. My aunt isn't here when I arrive, so Mom lets me inside. The last time I was over here the couch was draped in blankets and a pillow as Mom's makeshift bed. Now the living room furniture has been pushed slightly closer together and an air mattress rests against the far wall underneath a surrealist painting of three women playing a piano.

"How'd the sign swap go?" Mom asks, reaching around me to press the door closed. I smell her perfume, the same kind she's worn her whole life, and I realize that Aunt Bree's place doesn't smell like *home*. It smells like my mom.

"It was fine," I say, dropping the van keys on the kitchen island. "Some of the old signs broke when I took them out of the grass."

"They're going in the trash anyway," Mom says with a dismissive wave of her hand. "Did the homeowners see them? Did they say anything?"

"No. I don't think anyone knew I was there."

I'm not sure if it's disappointment or relief that flashes across my mom's eyes. Probably the first one. "Guess people will see them soon."

She pours us both a glass of sweet tea.

"You haven't cut your hair in a while," she says, reaching

up and touching my hair. "You want a pretty new style? I'll pay."

I look down and lift up a piece of my hair. The ends are scraggly and unkept, and my roots are much darker than they usually are at this time of year. Still, fancy hair seems like something people do when they have their life together. I shrug. "No, I'm fine."

"Let me know if you change your mind."

Mom turns up the music that's playing through a small but powerful speaker on the coffee table, then plops down on Aunt Bree's overstuffed denim couch. I like this new side of my mother. She's happy now. And for a long time she wasn't happy at all. I feel awful that it took seeing her happy to realize just how unhappy she had been.

But things are different now. Life is changing. I have to believe that it's all for the best.

The door to Aunt Bree's studio apartment opens and she walks in backwards, carrying a pizza box so large it barely fits through the door. "Howdy, loves," she says, kicking the door closed behind her. "Hope you're hungry."

The extra-large Brooklyn style cheese pizza is delicious. We eat it straight from the box like the fun single ladies we are. Mom comes alive in a new way when she's with Aunt Bree. I can totally picture how they were as teenagers, before Mom fell hard for my dad and promptly glued herself to his side.

"Oh! I almost forgot," Aunt Bree says, holding up a finger while she takes another bite of her pizza before dropping the half-eaten slice into the box. She walks over to the shelf next to her microwave and holds out a large felt pennant for Fault Line University. "Ta-da!"

I stare at my empty glass of sweet tea. "That's nice of you,

Aunt Bree, but it doesn't matter anymore, because I missed the acceptance date."

"You most certainly did not," Aunt Bree says before taking another bite of her pizza.

"I did," I say, feeling that ball of guilt and remorse rise up in my stomach like it does every time I think of my dream college. Of Mason. Of things that might have been. "May first was the deadline. It's already June now."

"You gonna tell her or should I?" Aunt Bree looks at my mom, who holds back a smile. The hairs on the back of my neck prickle. Aunt Bree gives me a devilish grin.

"Tell me what?" I say, looking to both of them.

Mom cracks first. "I sent in your acceptance."

"*We* sent in your acceptance," Aunt Bree says, grinning widely at her big sister. "You never signed out of my computer."

The air disappears from the room, taking all sounds with it until all I can hear is the pounding of my own heart. "I can go to my dream school?" My whole body feels alive, like I've just fallen into an electrical outlet. "I can go? *I'm going?*"

"You are absolutely going to your dream school," Mom says.

I stand up. No words come out.

"I should have told you sooner," Mom says, rushing over and hugging me so hard I can't breathe and I don't even mind. "We wanted to plan a fancy way to tell you, make it a big surprise, but then everything got so crazy."

"But... I'm already going to A&M..." I stutter. "And money... and..."

"Don't worry one bit," Aunt Bree says. "I sold a painting for an obscene amount of money." She wiggles her eyebrows. "It's enough to cover your first semester's tuition. Amber's got your room and board. Now, I can't promise I can pull that off for the rest of your college life, but I'll try."

I take several breaths. Pick up the pennant and run my fingers over the felt. Then I dive across the couch, my arm still around Mom's neck, my other reaching for my aunt. We collapse into a big hug and a fit of laughter.

"Thank you."

CHAPTER THIRTY-FOUR

I would never admit this to my beloved Dinosaur Valley state park, but Colorado is beyond beautiful. Mom and I had difficulty concentrating on the GPS as we took turns driving up Interstate 25 in Mom's car. We'd only planned a few road trip destinations this time, like the famed Red Rock Canyon and the breathtaking suspension bridge that crosses the Royal Gorge, but we added dozens more to our list of future road trip destinations. At home in Stonebrook, the ground is mostly flat, the horizon is boring, and the only hiking that can be found is around shopping malls. Everything in Colorado is stunning and three-dimensional and overflowing with the beauty of Mother Nature. I'm already in love.

Mom's car is actually my car now. She upgraded to a new SUV and gave me her car as a going-away-to-college gift. I've already decorated the back window with an FLU sticker.

After Mom helps me get settled into my dorm she will fly back home. Dad said he would come visit me soon. There was a brief talk of all three of us road-tripping it up here, but thankfully we all agreed that idea would be a huge failure.

Plus, I'm an adult now. I don't want to show up at college with both parents clinging to my side. We're not in Stonebrook, Texas anymore. I have new impressions to make. And while I love my parents, I'm tired of being known as their daughter first, and an independent person second.

I've already virtually met my new college roommate through email. Her name is Cayla and she's an engineering major from Oklahoma. She told me she loves sunflowers and candles, so when I was shopping for college stuff with Mom, I found the perfect candle to give her as a "welcome to college and please don't be a bad roommate" gift. It's a glass votive with three wicks and has sunflowers hand painted all around it. The wax smells like wildflowers, wood, and citrus. I can already imagine the scent filling up our dorm room.

I am eager to start my new college life and to dive into my favorite earthy subjects. I don't know what I'll do after I graduate, or what kind of person I'll be with a geoscience degree, but I'm so happy I get to figure it out on my own terms.

I guess I'm expecting something straight out of a teenage movie set, but real life college is pretty chill. The freshmen are all located in Connally Hall, a two-story dorm building that overlooks the mountains. Today and tomorrow are the official move in days and then college starts on Monday. I am only mildly freaking out. It's all new and surreal but it's not as scary as I imagined. It's actually thrilling.

My dorm room is on the second floor with an amazing view, *and* it's close to the parking lot. Score. Cayla isn't here yet, so Mom and I look around the small space, opening and closing drawers on the built-in dresser-bed combo and peeking in the empty closet. I don't need to look at her to know she's sharing in my giddy excitement.

"This is really cool," I say, dropping butt first onto my new bed. It's half the width of my bed at home and the mattress we bought came rolled up in a box that's still sitting on the floor, but that doesn't make it any less amazing.

"It is cool," Mom says, giving me one of her appraising smiles. "I'm so proud of you."

"I didn't really do anything." I glance out the small window, looking down at the parking lot. Beyond that lies a low mountain range, which I'm pretty sure is Mount Rock judging by the campus map. Mount Rock is where all the freshmen make their orientation hike, which takes place in a few hours.

"Yes you did," Mom says.

Turning back to her, I curl my lip in disagreement. "You and Aunt Bree sent in my acceptance. You both paid for this semester. You gave me the car to get here. Until I actually graduate, I haven't accomplished anything."

"You filled out the application in the first place," Mom says. "You got a great SAT score and wrote the essay. You've been prepping for this your entire life, Honey. You just maybe didn't realize it at first. I know I didn't. But I'm glad you're here."

"Will R&B be okay without me?" I ask. The family companies aren't technically R&B anymore now that they're split into two, but old habits die hard. Mom doesn't seem to care that I called it by the old name.

"We will be fine," she says. She reaches up and presses her palm to my cheek. It's a little cheesy, but it makes my heart feel all warm and cozy. I won't see her again until Thanksgiving, and after all we've been through lately, I know I'll miss her like crazy. "Come on," Mom says, walking over to the big mattress box. "My ride to the airport gets here in an hour. Let's get you unpacked."

One time Mom told me the story of my first day of kindergarten. She said Jill had been a blubbering mess, crying her mascara off on the drive to school before she had ever even said goodbye to Luca. But my mom wasn't emotional about it, and she didn't understand why parents made such a big deal about kindergarten. It was just school, and it's not like her kid wouldn't come home at the end of the day. I don't really remember my first day of school, but Mom says she and Jill walked Luca and me into our class. While Jill cried like a water fountain saying goodbye to Luca, Mom just hugged me and told me to have a good day.

She said it wasn't until she walked out to her car that it all hit her at once and she had no idea why, but she burst into tears. Emotions are weird like that.

I don't cry at all as I walk my mom to the taxi that picks her up for her trip back home. When the car drives away and I'm left standing here in a brand new state a thousand miles from home, I keep expecting to burst into tears like my mom had done all those years ago when I went to kindergarten. She's probably crying in the taxi right now. Tears must not be on the agenda for me today, because all I feel is an excitement so electrifying my whole body feels lit up with possibilities. I did it. I'm here.

Rushing back to my dorm, I prop my phone on the dresser, set the self-timer and then step back from the camera, holding out my arms and making a "can you believe it?" face. I send the photo to Luca. *Made it to college!*

You look smarter already he replies with an emoji that's wearing nerdy glasses.

I smile. Luca and I are going to be just fine. Not as lovers, but as friends.

After orientation, my roommate Cayla and I lose track of each other while we're searching for our boulder. The smooth round rock is only about ten pounds and the size of a bag of flour, but they call them Capstone Boulders since they are symbolic of the three massive boulders that decorate the front of the campus. Those were set in place by a crane when the school was established fifty years ago. This school is rooted in several traditions, one of which is the tradition of incoming freshman carrying a boulder up Mount Rock and leaving it there until graduation.

A woman wearing an FLU polo shirt hands me a Sharpie from a big box and I bend down to write my name on my chosen boulder.

"Can I borrow that when you're done?"

My heart skips a beat from hearing the one person who hasn't left my thoughts since I arrived in town. I knew he'd find me before I found him. That's just his style.

"That depends," I say, standing up and snapping the cap back on my marker and holding it out to him. He's wearing black skinny jeans and a maroon long-sleeved flannel that makes him look ridiculously huggable. I swallow back those urges and fix him with a sarcastic stare. "Are you going to annoy me with scientific facts about the mountain range?"

Mason takes the marker. "I will *entertain* you with scientific facts about the mountain range," he says slowly, the side of his lips curving into a grin. "But only if you want me to."

I roll my eyes. "You're only going to get smarter and more annoying as we go through college, huh?"

"Smarter? Yes. More handsome? Also yes."

I knock him in the shoulder with my own. "That's not what I said."

He grins. "You didn't have to say it."

Kneeling down, he writes *Mason Ramos* in large blocky letters across the top of his boulder. "So," he says, rising back up on his feet. "Are you making the hike now or waiting until after dark? My roommate said a lot of people wait until night because the sky looks amazing. There's no light pollution here."

"I'm going now," I say, looking down at my rock. I gaze back up into his dark eyes. "I think I want to do this on my own."

I know I shouldn't feel guilty, but I do, a little bit. Hiking up a small mountain next to Mason could be all kinds of romantic. But that is not why I uprooted my whole life to come to this college.

He nods. "Want to meet for dinner? We could head to the cafeteria and see what college food tastes like."

"Yeah. That sounds fun." I smile. He smiles back.

One day I will tell him exactly what it took for me to get here. Something tells me he will listen, and he won't be judgmental or weird about it. Something tells me Mason Ramos will wait as long as it takes for me to decide I'm ready to kiss him again.

The warm autumn air is easy to breathe as I make my way up Mount Rock. The gross humidity of Texas is something I'm happy to leave behind in my hometown. I carry my chosen ten pound boulder in my arms like a baby while I walk, sometimes shifting it around to get more comfortable. The hike is long and the trail is narrow, but fairly smooth as far as hiking up a mountain goes. I don't think I ever hiked in Texas, but I might be doing it a lot more now that there are an infinite number of trails to explore. My shins start to ache and I think I have a gnarly blister forming on my big toe, but I make it up here in just under an hour.

The view is spectacular. I wander a bit further away from the other freshmen who are placing their boulders among the hundreds that came before us. In our orientation they had spoken about how this boulder was a representation of the hard work we'll put into our college years. That it's a place-holder of all that's to come, all that we are to achieve, and it'll be here waiting when we come back to get it after graduation.

I gaze around at the boulders that decorate this vast peak. Some are painted, or decorated in glitter. Some have names written in bold lettering, while others have chicken scratch you can barely make out. Mine is somewhere in the middle. I used the black Sharpie and wrote my full name, simply in all caps, across the top. Honey Bree Blackwell.

Kneeling down, I smooth some of the gravel away with my hand, and then carefully, as if this rock really does contain a bit of my soul, I set it down on top of the mountain. I stare at it for a moment, then stand up and brush my hands off on the front of my shorts before shoving them in my back pockets. Gazing out at the gorgeous landscape before me, I take in the beauty of this new state. I close my eyes and listen to the sounds of nature, of birds chirping and wind rustling through the brush.

I have my whole future waiting for me.

It starts now.

ACKNOWLEDGMENTS

First and always: Chris, Hallee, Katie, and Felicia. You're the spine glue to my pages. The dust jacket to my hardcover. The rolling cart to my stack of library books. What I'm trying to say is you all hold my life together. Nova and Quinn, you are both very, very good dogs. (As always.)

Deirdre Hall, my bookish bestie in a million ways, thank you for always being there and for not blocking my email yet. Abigail Johnson, you always fill me with enthusiasm and make me remember that I actually love writing. All the thanks and love in the world to my writer friends, the only people who truly *get it*: Jenn Acres, Ann Rose, Patricia Tighe, Jennifer DiGiovanni, Tammy Takaishi, Karole Cozzo, Lynn Painter (Fold in the cheese!), Melanie Hooyenga, Becky Wallace, Gina Ciocca, Rachel Harris — I'm so grateful for you all.

Sarah Davis, Karen Downs, Marcia Woodell, Ellie Mae, Gabriela Nunez, thank you for being my biggest cheerleaders! I'm honored to have you in my life.

A million thanks to the teachers and librarians who work tirelessly as an advocate of books. And a super-size thank you to Reba Gordon.

Thanks to book bloggers who find books they love and make sure everyone knows about it. Belle Ellrich in particular. You're amazing!

And to you, reader. Thank you for reading my book. I hope you'll tell your friends about it.

ABOUT THE AUTHOR

Cheyanne Young is a native Texan with a fear of cold weather and a coffee addiction that probably needs an intervention. She loves books, sarcasm, and collecting nail polish. She writes books for young adults (and the young adults at heart), often while covered in dog hair.

Follow her online:
www.CheyanneYoung.com

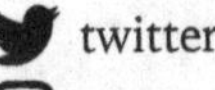 twitter.com/NormalChey
 instagram.com/NormalChey

How far would you go for your best friend?

The day Raquel has been dreading for months has finally arrived. Sasha, her best friend in the whole world — *the* best friend in the whole world — has died of cancer. Raquel can't imagine life without her. She's overwhelmed and brokenhearted.

But can Raquel remain true to herself while also honoring her friend's final wish?

After months of therapy in the school's Breakup Support Group, the pieces of Isla's heart are finally healed. And now she just handed it over to a guy who only knows how to break them.